PART TWO

OMISSION

FATE'S BITE SERIES

MY WIFE. MY FEMALE. MY PRECIOUS ONE.

ELENA M. REYES

SUMMARY

Anaya:

"Hello, little mate."
Three sweet words, and they eviscerated the very foundation I once stood upon.
Because I'd resigned myself to a life of sadness and pain without a mate. Without love. Each day, I'd been slowly dying inside under my father's oppressive hold—the constant pain his lies caused—while he arranged my marriage to a man I both loathed and feared.
My people turned a blind eye to this. They didn't care.
And yet, one look into the Wiccan King's possessive eyes, and my world came alive with color.
In this male, I found love. Acceptance. A home.
Three things I will fight to keep. Will bleed for.

Leonardo:

Their biggest mistake was touching what is mine.
This pure and innocent soul given to me by the Gods that I treasure above all else. Above duty. Above vendettas yet to be fulfilled

because nothing matters more than her happiness, and if I must eradicate an entire kingdom to protect her, so mote it be.

I wear her mark on my cock with pride. My female is the only one I'd bend a knee for.

I'M A KING.

A PROTECTOR.

I'm irrevocably tied to her until my last dying breath, and even then, I'll still be hers.

ACKNOWLEDGMENTS

For all the bookish girlies who love an OTT possessive alpha male who spoils his Queen while spanking her ass and calling her his: *"Good girl."*

TRIGGER WARNINGS:

This book contains dark elements that some readers might find triggering. This man is brutal and unapologetic, please read at your own discretion.

Contains:

Explicit Violence (GORE)
Explicit Language
Death & Torture
Biting/Mating Mark
Abusive family
Misogynistic Male Family Members
Possessive Anti-Hero
Threatening of FMC
Abuse of FMC by Villain (Not Sexual)
Some Blood Play/Licking During Sex (Bite or Cut)
Fated Mates
Drugging/Poisoning of FMC by Villain
Kidnapping Of Child, No Harm. Just A Scare

PART TWO

OMISSION

FATE'S BEAUTIES

ELENA M. REYES

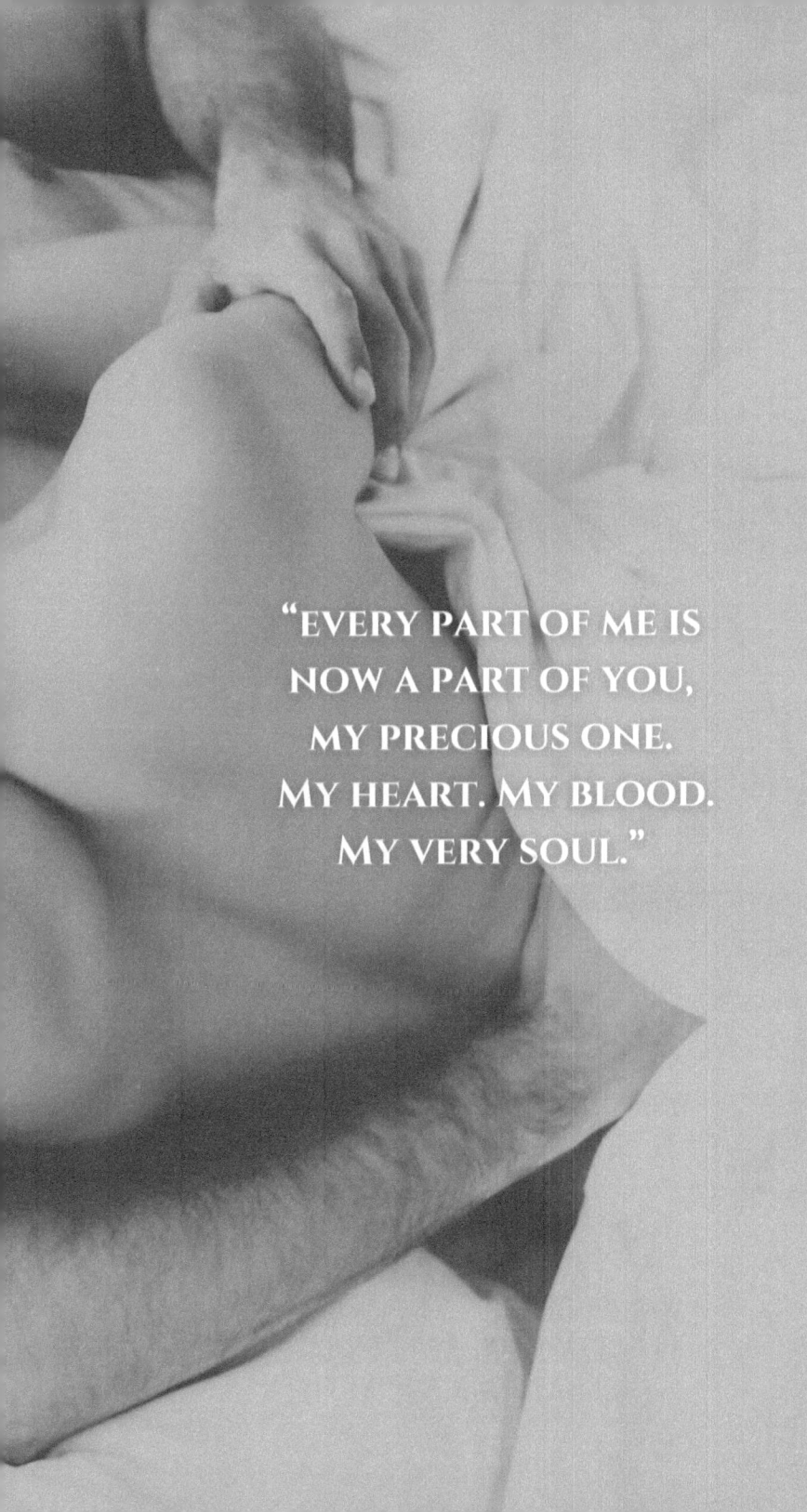

"EVERY PART OF ME IS
NOW A PART OF YOU,
MY PRECIOUS ONE.
MY HEART. MY BLOOD.
MY VERY SOUL."

OMISSION

FATE'S BITE SERIES

playlist

BLACK HOLE SUN BY SOUNDGARDEN
INTO THE DARKNESS BY THE PHANTOMS
SHADOW OF THE DAY BY LINKIN PARK
WELCOME TO THE FIRE BY WILLYECHO
TURNING PAGE BY SLEEPING AT LAST
I COULD FALL IN LOVE BY SELENA
CALLING YOU BY BLUE OCTOBER
AUTEUR BY SAINT MESA
I WANNA BE YOURS BY ARCTIC MONKEYS
BETWEEN RAINDROPS BY LIFEHOUSE &
NATASHA BEDINGFIELD

PART TWO

OMISSION
FATE'S BITE SERIES

playlist

EVERYTHING BY LIFEHOUSE
MI VERDAD BY MANA & SHAKIRA
FAVORITO BY CAMILO
PHOTOGRAPH BY ED SHEERAN
BUILT BY NATIONS BY GRETA VAN FLEET
ANIMAL I HAVE BECOME BY THREE DAYS GRACE
NIGHT VIVE BY SKYFALL BEATS
HIGHWAY TUNE BY GRETA VAN FLEET
OCEAN BY KAROL G
YOUNG AND BEAUTIFUL BY LANA DEL REY

"YOUR MATE WILL BE
YOUR PEACE. HE WILL BE
EVERYTHING YOU'VE
EVER DREAMED OF...
SWEET, CARING, AND
WILL PUT YOU ABOVE ALL
ELSE. INCLUDING HIS
HATRED. HIS NEED FOR
VENGEANCE."

MEMORIES

Anaya

LAST CONVERSATION WITH HER MOTHER...

"**C**ome and sit with me for a minute, Anaya," Mother calls out as I pass her open doorway, a now-empty tea tray in my hand. I'd been given the *honor* of preparing for, and then attending to, the needs of my father's sister while she visited the fae court.

Silla arrived a few days after being summoned by our king.

I welcomed her and then the elders, my grandfather included, by serving them a le goûter upon arriving. Just as I *graciously* hosted an ostentatious dinner later that evening, my lips not moving from their permanently curved, yet demure smile. No teeth shown. Face relaxed. Always saying *oui* to whatever ridiculous request these guests had because they couldn't serve themselves something as simple as a glass of water.

It's beneath them, but not me. I'm a prisoner, my gilded cage full of sharp edges—the metal formed into thorns and blades that cut at every turn. My title is nothing more than a life-long sentence under the guise of nobility. I'm seen as an object, not a person, and used to further push our king's moral beliefs.

To most members of the fae kingdom, we're the picture-perfect family.

We're led by a stern, yet loving monarch who prides himself on the façade he's erected over the remains of my mother's legacy, a tired queen saved by a loving mate and eldest son who stepped in to take care of those under her aegis.

You are nothing but a pawn I move at my discretion. You have no voice or choice; remember that, my child.

A lesson I learned the hard way multiple times throughout the years via warnings, punishments, and then snarled promises, the latter of which was to permanently take my maman from me.

Because a good and proper princess:

Is bound by duty.

Serves her people.

Has the privilege to be seen, *never* heard, and admired by all for her selflessness.

Furthermore, these traits can be explained as part of our royal etiquette, but I know better. It's a way to further push our king's misogynistic views, and they apply to all females unless you're his sister.

All of his devout followers are men. Every high-ranking member of the court is a male.

Aunt Silla's presence filled the palace with a buzz that felt *off.* The halls were overpowered by a tinge of heaviness I tried to evade while she gallivanted as if she were a true member of the royal family. While our true queen went into a *forced* seclusion.

Maman was hidden from sight while our guest believed she was recuperating from an unknown ailment. A lie.

No one questioned it, though. Don't think my father's devout followers care.

Silla's stay on fae territory lasted a little over twenty-four hours, and she wreaked havoc in her wake. Each minute here was spent in private discussion with our elders, the military, and lastly, our king— I haven't slept yet.

Mother hasn't either. Not because she's sick or tired, but because of her punishment sessions before dinner and after, while the rest of the visitors enjoyed a cup of coffee. While they ate a decadent dessert and my aunt smiled, our father retired to his office with my mother, whose head hung low.

"You will stand here and not make a sound or intervene, my child. Do not make this worse on your poor mother and force my hand, or I'll make her bleed this time. Understood?"

"Yes, Father." My voice is low and my throat feels tight—eyes becoming glassy—but I force the tears back.

"Very good." The hint of pride in his tone makes me want to scream, but that also can't happen. I'm trapped. Forced to lower my head and give in to his command, no matter how much I want to rebel and hurt him. *"Once I exit, you will count to ten and then attend to Amelia. Get her unseen to her chambers. Do not disappoint me."*

Then there's silence. Utter stillness.

For a few minutes, there's nothing until it begins.

Low. Slow. A whimper turned sharp cry as the minutes tick by, and her apologies follow each pain-filled sound.

"I'm so sorry for Silla's displeasure, mon cherie. I'll do better."

"I wish to be the queen you deserve, mon roi."

"What can I do to make this up to you? You deserve better, mon beau."

Again, there's a beat of silence and the hiccuping sob from my queen. "I'll personally make amends for missing such an important dinner with your sister. Present her with a priceless jewel on the queen's behalf."

Each cry broke my heart. Her responses—her scent—gave away her fear, not remorse.

It tinged everything, including our connection. And I'm sure I'm not the only one who felt it. Other faes had to have too, even if they no longer understood what the sudden discomfort filling their chest meant. The disconnection between her and them is a large abyss now, and while the ember is still glowing inside, it's un-nurtured. Dimmed.

Queen Amelia is being written out of our history.

Then, the final nail in her coffin was the so-called lack of *Silla's* favorite mint soap in her en-suite bath.

Another lie told.

Every single offense was a lie, especially her love of mint. That woman is particular to the scent of roses—floral anything. Moreover, I stocked that bathroom myself. Inspected every inch of her suite to appease my father and gain reprieve for my mother, but that was a fool's hope.

Maman bore the brunt of his mental lashes, fifteen each time, one after another; a physical and mentally painful experience, yet no marks were left behind.

There is no proof of abuse. Nothing that could ever be pinned on him.

Silla's disdain for my mother has never made sense to me; literal repulsion is clear as day on her face whenever she visits, but it's without cause. Mother is always polite when in her presence, ignores every snide comment, and gifts graciously, while the woman doesn't deserve such care.

And while she's never been outright cruel, there's something off in her eyes when she looks at me. It's not hate, but more like...*fear.* Trepidation.

A little bit of care, which makes no sense. Why is Silla wary of me?

It's something I'd been questioning while bringing my mother her favorite tea, a drink my brother stole before I could reach her room. Ruben doesn't like tea and my father abhors my mother's choice with its notes of black currant and vanilla, but the action was meant to simply ruin my gesture.

Confirmed a second later when he tossed the cup against the wall where it shattered and the contents spilled all over the marble flooring.

"Come, child, we must be quick."

"Yes, Maman." I keep my voice low, a near whisper as to not hurt her head. Her mate's mental attack left her a whimpering mess both times, the residual proof of his abuse clear in her eyes. They're sad and glassy; the tears that gather at the corners will never fall, but that's a testament to her strength. *She protects me any way she can, even if it's to her detriment.* "Is there anything I can get for you?"

"My sole purpose in this life before I go is to prepare you for what's to come, Anaya. That you're ready. That you're strong enough to rise and—"

"Are you leaving again?" Because I know the story. I may only be sixteen summers, but it's a tale spoken about by the court's female servants whenever the king isn't around. They don't hide it from me, though. Some whisper it as a warning, while others as a hero's folklore.

Because those of a lower status aren't treated like the elders or guards, more so if you're a woman.

They see things. They live with the brutality those like Brice, my father's general—who thinks highly of himself—unleash on their male family members. They clean wounds and stitch them up while fighting back tears because they aren't allowed.

Not in our kingdom. We're lucky to have a ruler like King Larue.

"One day, but not like before." A short sentence, and yet it carries so much agony. Can feel her regret. "And that's why I need you to listen, and never repeat what I'm about to tell you to anyone." Wincing, Maman palms her forehead with her left hand, while with the right, she tugs me to sit beside her on the bed. Her body shakes with the effort, her face pinched tight from the pain. "Promise me, Aya."

Her use of my nickname, one only she uses, causes my heart to clench. For my nerves to heighten; I hide it the best I can behind an honest smile. "I promise."

"You're a true queen." Her bottom lip trembles a bit, and she takes a few minutes to regain her composure. She's looking toward the door, the points of her ears twitching as if listening for movement outside in the hall. There's no one there, and once satisfied, Maman turns her violet eyes—so much like mine—back to me. "I hope one day you look back on this conversation with fondness and know how much I love you, my child. You're the only thing I've done right in this world."

"Maman, what's going on? You're worrying me."

"Hush, ma princesse. There's nothing for you to fear." I want to argue that, tell her we should leave together like she did a century ago before my birth, but the words die on my tongue when she shakes her head. The action causes her to wince, and I forget her past pleas and the promises I've made to never use my powers; I lift a hand and place it over her head. Feed her a bit of my strength while my skin glows in the dim lighting.

A move that would be easy to see even from a distance, the air around us vibrates with my magic—I'm healing what I can, and fast, because you never know who lurks on our royal grounds. Males and those of status wouldn't hesitate to sell me out, turn me over to be used by my father as his personal healer, while they reap a reward for such loyalty.

Then, you have those who are desperate to change their ranking.

Not because they're evil or uncaring, but to escape. Protect themselves.

If anyone knew I'm a healer—

"Stop," Mom says, her voice a lot steadier after only a few seconds, and she pulls my hand down. Keeps it in hers while giving it a small squeeze. There's a bit of reproach in her expression, but it's mixed with appreciation and I smile at her. Won't deny that I'm a bit faint now, that my body wants to shut down and sleep, but I force myself to stay alert. *It's worth it to see her with more color in her cheeks.* "I'm good, child. Don't ever do that again."

"I'd never leave you to suffer if I can help."

"And that's my biggest fear." At the confusion on my face, Mom sighs. "I don't want you to heal me, sweetheart. Don't put yourself in his path. Your father must never know of your gifts."

"But I felt the—"

"Poison?" Her tone is so flat. Detached and resigned. "You felt it?"

"Yes."

"Then let it be."

"Maman!" I whisper yell, so angry she'd even suggest that. "How can you expect—"

"I demand it as your queen."

"Mother, please don't."

"I will do what I must." As a true royal from the original blood-line, her word is above my father's, something he knows and hates. It's why he threatens her with hurting me if she doesn't comply with his authority while playing the same mind games with me. To keep us docile in front of every fae subject. To keep his chauvinistic agendas growing. "Not something I like doing, but don't force my hand, Aya. Trust that what I do, I do with your well-being at heart."

"Who?"

"The better question is—are your senses dulled?"

"No." Swallowing hard, I close my eyes for a second, just enough to gather myself before meeting her unwavering stare. "I think I'm just used to it."

"Surrounded by it."

"Yes."

"Then you know the answer." The low chatter of someone outside in the hall filters into the room, and we stay quiet as the women complain about the mess made by my brother, Ruben.

They're diligent and gone within minutes, yet our ears stay perked up until their scents dissipate and Maman is satisfied they're gone. "We've wasted too much time. Please listen to everything I have to say and try to save your questions for another day. Can you do that for me?"

"I vow it."

"Thank you." The expression on her face is one of peace while she squeezes my hand tight. Her room is cold and I shiver, something Maman picks up on quickly, and her pure white wings extend before the one on my side shifts to surround me. A hug from our mother queen and I snuggle in close, laying my head on her shoulder. Exhaustion is starting to become a problem for me, but I force myself to pay attention when she starts talking again. Her voice is low. "Pure-hearted faes are easier to distinguish when you know what you're looking for, my little Aya. Those with the dark sickness reek of it—it clings to their being—and you need to heed that warning, young one. Those high-priced sentences are paid for by their magical essence, rotting them from within for wielding forbidden magic."

"Only the fae, Maman?"

"Not another question," she chides softly, "but no." Her face is sad, and she swallows hard—the hurt she carries for the sins of her people weighs heavily, but she does so silently. A true queen never complains. Never falters. "Every breathing creature can be tempted, and those that fall prey carry the pungent note."

"But you—"

Ignoring my inability to remain quiet, she tsks before carrying on. "That same magic is being used on me, by your father. He feeds me a dose every day via my morning duties as his mate. I hear his low incantations, smell the vileness, and know my time is coming." Maman lifts her shoulder a bit, so I look up and now find her violet eyes...*happy*. Proud. "They might win against me, ma princesse, but not you. You are stronger and fiercer than what you believe and will one day rule more than one kingdom with a male as pure-hearted as you. And that man, my love, he will sweep you off your feet."

"How do you—"

I'm cut off this time by the snarled tone of my father; he's yelling at someone, and it's coming from the end of the hallway. Mother's chambers are a floor below his and if he's gracing us with his presence, it's because I'm needed to play host or finish my duties as the dutiful daughter while his *unwell* mate rests.

"Your mate will be your *peace*. He will be everything you've ever dreamed of..." Mother's words are rushed now, an almost unintelligible whisper "...sweet, caring, and will put you above all else. Including his hatred. His need for vengeance."

"His hatred, Maman? Vengeance?"

Yet before she can answer, her bedroom door is opened wide and my father, the king of all faes, stands at the entrance. His stare is accusatory. Always distrustful. "There you are, Anaya. Your grandfather has been looking for you."

"My apologies, my king. I came to ask Maman a question."

"A question?" His tone to someone unaware of his cruelty is pleasant, but I hear the tinge of a threat. "What question?"

"Woman issues." The lie slips from me easily, and it helps that his mate remains at ease beside me. It's also convenient that he *can't* handle something as simple as a menstrual cycle.

"Which ones?"

"Pain and heaviness during my time of—"

"Enough." End of. He doesn't want to hear anymore.

It works for me. Keeps his mate safe for the time being.

Because Father can never find out about our private conversations or her warnings.

He'd take her from me, otherwise.

CHAPTER 1

Anaya

For the first time in my life, I understand the true meaning of the word *peace*.

It's a deep sense of nothingness while being overwhelmingly everything all in the same breath. It's a comforting silence that stretches and fills every inch of the space surrounding us while a blanket of warmth protects my heart and soothes my soul. While my lungs expand on a quiet sigh, the scent of chocolate and cloves settles inside me.

I've never felt so safe. So free.

With my king, I'm weightless and full of hope. There are no background noises or interruptions. No threats looming close—no need to fear my present or future—because everything outside of lying in my male's arms has lost all meaning.

He is all I hear. All I see.

He's the overwhelming essence—the truest definition of love—filling my being while simultaneously erasing all my worries. Knitting together all those open wounds, the proof of my prior subjugation and life filled with pain, that now no longer registers.

Then, there's the rhythmic rise and fall of his chest while the thumping of his resting heart lulls me into a plane of pure satisfaction that pulls a low purr from me. It's a sound I've never made before him; a tiny little mewl that expresses the unadulterated happiness currently flowing through every molecule of my fae DNA.

Especially when he tightens his hold on me every few minutes. When his bare, semi-hard cock twitches against my thigh.

"No night clothes for either of us, precious one."

"But what about when—"

Leo *places a warm fingertip over my lips, his smile so sweet. All for me.* "I want to feel you, Anaya. All of you. There will be no clothing worn inside our private chambers—nothing to keep me away—it's the king's decree. An order. One I'll test more than once, even while we're out in public because I'll always simply need you."

Leonardo's asleep beside me, but that doesn't diminish our connection as he's placed my naked body half-strewn high across his broad chest while one of his hands palms my right asscheek possessively. Grip strong, his fingers dig into my flesh every few minutes as he pets me and then returns to his slumber.

Over and over again.

It's the sweetest torture.

An unconscious act, I know this, but I also can't help but preen under his open need for me.

To feel me. To have me close. To own me.

"My precious one." It's a deep, yet sleep-filled rumble from his chest. The sound's low and a bit garbled, yet I understand each word clearly. Accept them as the gift they are and tilt my head up, finding his face pinched and brows furrowed. It shows his frustration over something—the bond between us clamoring with an unfulfilled need —before two thick fingers dig deeper and I whimper.

Not from pain, but from desire.

Moreover, the sound soothes something in my Wiccan king. That tightness lessens immediately, his face appearing almost boyish in his rest, and I bite back another wanton sound—I don't want him to wake up just yet—while the pads of his fingers skim from one side to the other. Leo does this three times, tracing the roundness of each cheek, back and forth, before settling over the cleft.

There he taps a few times; Leo's playing a tune only he can hear in his sleep. Something that escalates from sweet to dirty on the next sweep as he pushes against the parted flesh.

At first, I freeze, hunger warring with the unease of the unknown. I'd lost my virginity just a few hours ago, but the pressure feels *good*. Exciting. Moreover, the pulse that travels through the touch of mates—this electrical current that pleasures every cell in my body— is currently thrumming against the erogenous zone, and I welcome it.

My king's touch.

The heat from his skin.

With each shiver he pulls from me, the goosebumps that rise across my sensitive flesh, I find myself pressing into his grip. Something he approves of, if the low growl in his chest is anything to go by.

My eyes never leave his face while he explores, though. I follow his unconscious petting and part my legs just enough to make it easier to reach what we both desire. Because I want this. My nerves don't deter me or alter my desire for this man to own every piece of me. Just like the soreness, the imprint of his thickness from our earlier lovemaking doesn't abate my hunger.

Each hole will bear his signature of ownership.

Each drop of my arousal is the property of King Leonardo Moore.

I vowed this the moment my fangs pierced his cock, leaving

behind my mating mark. One he's thanked me profusely for with each earlier kiss, stroke, and grunted praise.

And I've never felt so loved. So purely wanted for simply being *me*.

Not because I'm a fae princess.

Not because of potential political gain.

No. This wonderful male made my first time beautiful and all about me.

Arching a bit more, I chase the next strum of his fingers and I'm rewarded by a slow sensual caress from hole to hole. He spreads my slickness, pressing a little harder, and the hard cock against my thigh jerks while a large pearl-like drop slides over my skin.

Its descent is like a slow caress that only serves to heighten the burning in my veins.

"Oh Gods," I moan low, unable to stop the words or the wanton tone. And as if he's heard me, my king slips a finger inside my still-tender pussy to the first knuckle. He doesn't press it. Instead, Leo keeps it in place while his muscles tense for a moment, letting me know the king of all Wiccans is awake.

Neither of us moves, either. We don't say a word as my wetness soaks his hand.

His eyes remain closed, yet his lids never cease their movement and his nostrils flare—while that sinful mouth tugs up at the corners, a smile that's just as deadly as the rest of him.

"Fuck, how I want you, my precious one." He slides that thick digit in a little more, the fingernail of his other hand biting into the flesh of my thigh that's stretched over his hip. Spreading me further. Giving himself full access. Something he takes advantage of and begins a torturous slide in and out with his finger—almost leisurely —while I'm clenching and breathing hard. Near panting. "How sore are you?"

"I'd never deny myself being with you."

At my response, his eyes open and they're heated blues. A little sleepy still, but the hunger is open and palpable. "As much as those words are a beautiful gift, Anaya, I don't want to hurt you."

"You'd destroy me if you said no."

"Fuck, sweetheart." Finger drenched in me, Leo slips it out and returns to my puckered hole. He doesn't enter, but instead circles twice and starts all over again. And again. It's maddening and amazing and I push against his hand without conscious thought, but he doesn't take it any further. "Tell me what you want, and it's yours. Anything you want, love."

"You. Just you."

"You've had me since the day you took your first breath. I've always belonged to my mate." And if my words a few seconds ago pleased him, *Leo's* fill me with a contradicting range of emotions that violently converge and leave me filled with pride, yet a bit *jealous.*

It's the wrong time to deal with this, but I can't control these storming reactions.

I've been docile all my life and almost died because of that flaw. My brother, a crowned prince brought up with the knowledge he was a king among the fae, tried to take my life. And in those few moments, when the poison took hold and I fought through the pain to come back to my mate, I vowed to never again ignore my instincts.

And right now, even as he continues to soothingly pet me, they're blaring with warning. Something I *need* to remember.

While Leonardo may have never wanted another—of that, I have no doubt—I'm reminded then of Chiara's unresolved behavior the day he brought me to his kingdom. Of the possessive way she looked at the male lying beneath me every time she was in his presence.

Of her blatant contempt for me. How she hates me while coveting what's mine.

As if she has a right to him.

I don't understand why this is bothering me *now*. It shouldn't matter after I've marked him and we've mated with each other, but for some reason, it slams into the forefront of my mind, holding me captive.

"Look at me, precious one." There's concern coming from his side of the bond; he's unhappy, but I don't acknowledge it. *Not yet.* Just like I'm unaware of my eyes leaving his face or when my fangs drop, because I'm mesmerized by a single bead of red that falls onto his right pectoral. I'm following its slow track across his skin, and while a minor sting comes from my top lip and the area is wet, I can't pull away.

Pure, unadulterated pride flames inside my chest as the sanguine drop pools at the center of his torso and begins to dry. Another mark. Another emotion battling for my attention, and this one wins momentarily.

Its hold is short-lived.

Just enough to send my love through the bond that connects us. A tug my king responds to, his force near staggering, but then I'm back to *her.*

To him. I'm being pulled by memories and vacillating between the emotions attached to each: love, desire—and anger. *Jealousy* and *darkness.*

This possessiveness is so unlike me. I've grown up giving without ever taking, but it's something I find myself accepting without question. It's now as much a part of me as breathing is—just as my love for him will always burn bright during our time walking this earth, and the centuries beyond.

However, the darkness I understand on a different level. Recognize the familiarity.

Tilting my head, I take note of the way the blueish tint in my blood contrasts against my king's flesh, mixing with his scent. I study the saccharine marker as a thought runs through my mind. Another recollection, this one is from my childhood: my mother's words and warnings.

"Pure-hearted faes are easier to distinguish when you know what you're looking for, my little Aya. Those with the dark sickness reek of it—it clings to their being—and you need to heed that warning, young one. Those high-priced sentences are paid for by their

magical essence, rotting them from within, for wielding forbidden magic."

"Only the fae, Maman?"

"No. Every breathing creature can be tempted, and those that fall prey carry the pungent note."

She gave me some hard truths about my father that day. She also gave me hope.

What to watch out for, and it makes sense now why this memory is important.

Because I finally understand what Maman meant by saying my mate is my *peace*.

And, how others can be tempted by power. Darkness.

That witch—

"Anaya, look at me." The sharp command pulls me from my thoughts, and my eyes snap to Leo's. His stare is penetrating, almost reproachful, and I don't like it. Hate the look of disappointment on his face. "I'd never look at another woman, my love."

"I know this, Leo. There's just something that—"

"No one could measure to the perfection that is my fae queen. Do you understand that, precious one? That no other being on this planet could ever hold my heart?" I nod in response, but that earns me a sharp smack across my right asscheek. It stings, then settles into a warmth that spreads in the most delicious way. It causes a rush of wetness to slip from me and onto his skin. "Use your words."

"Yes." A little more than breathless. An unconscious whine slips and my hips gyrate against his hold. *I'm not angry with you, my king. Just remembered something important.* "I believe you."

"Good girl." Two words spoken in that sleep-rumbled tone mixed with his natural deep timbre, and I melt against him. Can't help but lower my face to his, our lips hovering while goosebumps rise across my sensitive skin. "Now kiss me, Anaya. I promise we'll talk after." *Whatever's bothering you, I will fix it. Whatever you need, I'm here.*

Our connection thrums with his love and sincerity. There's also worry there, but his need to reassure me overrides everything, and I'm quickly pinned beneath him. A tiny squeal slips from me, my heart beating fast at the move, but the sound only excites him.

He's nestled between my thighs, hard and throbbing against my slick flesh. Then, there's the way his nostrils flare and he bares his teeth, a tell I've picked up on—Leo's need for me is uncontrollable, and I welcome his hunger with my own.

I'll never get over how good it feels to connect with you like this. I've said this to him before. Our private link is like a pleasurable caress to my senses and completely different from what I'd been subjugated to by my father. There's no pain when we communicate like this—just sweetness. It fills me with peace and security. *How each touch is better than the last.*

"I can't fucking live without you." *Just like I'll spend the rest of my life protecting your heart, precious one.* His face is inches from mine; I breathe in his every exhale while licking my lips. It's then I realize my fangs are still out, and a blush sweeps across my cheeks. The heat almost makes me cover my face with my hands; my hands leave his arms for a second, but that's as far as they go.

He gives a small shake of the head and I stop, placing them back on his skin. An action Leo approves of, the praise clear in his heated blue eyes—the way this powerful male breathes me in and then groans before pecking me once. "You're perfection, Anaya. My female."

"And I'm going to need more than that, mon amour. *Make me yours,* my king."

CHAPTER 2
LEONARDO

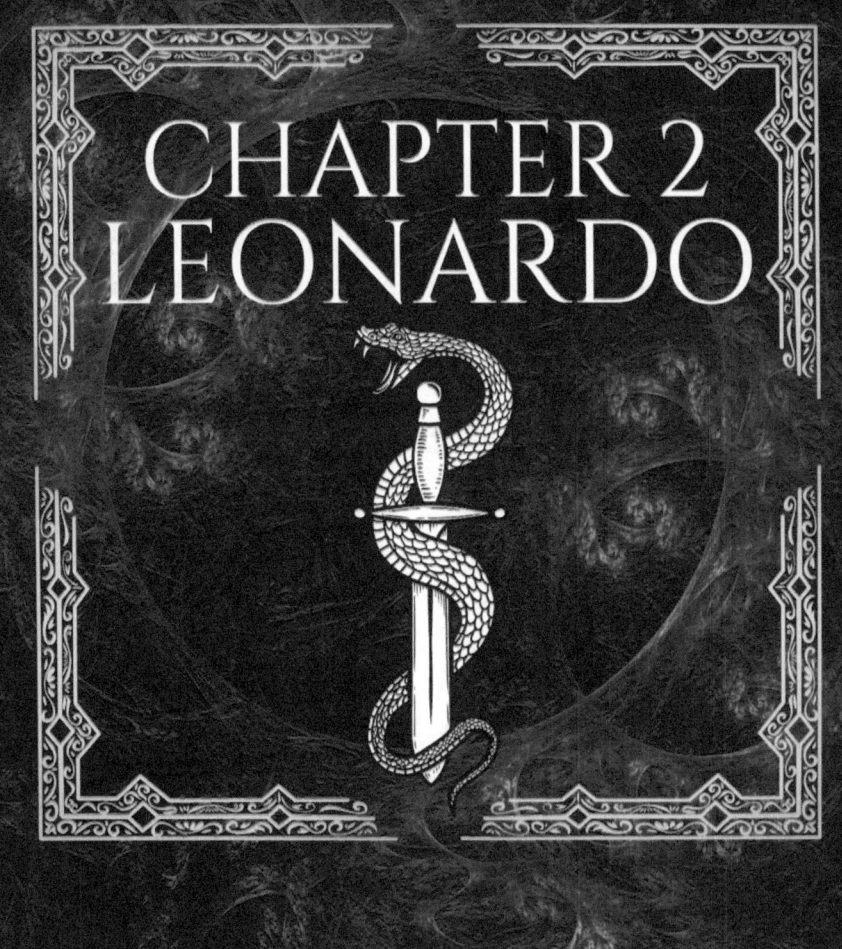

"**Y**ou've never been anything but mine, my precious one. I'm here for you. Was born to love you," I growl before slanting my mouth over hers, taking what I need. And while we need to talk and fix whatever put that look on her face a few seconds ago, I'll start by reassuring her first.

Physically. Emotionally. Then I'll eradicate the issue:

What's left of her family and Silla. Whoever poses a threat to our union.

The constant desire I feel for this beautiful woman goes beyond hunger or rationality—there's so much more to us, and no one will threaten this connection.

This bond feels deeper. Is all-consuming.

As if I'd owned her heart for centuries and her hand had been held by mine for just as long.

When I see Anaya, I'm reminded of the happiness on my parents' faces when they were in each other's presence. Of the times my father explained that my mother was his home and his peace.

The love of a good woman cannot be measured by gold, Leo. Nothing will compare to the way a simple smile will center you or how the moments of pain—inevitable darkness—fade as you seek solace in her arms.

And while my fae queen is all those things and more to me; his explanation of what a true mating is, and what *we* are, doesn't do us justice. We transcend. We burn too bright to contain.

A moan slips from Anaya and into my mouth, causing me to hiss in response as that slick slit rubs over my cock, the engorged head bumping her clit with each stroke. Something she rewards me for by gifting me those precious little mewls, each one a bit higher in pitch, and I flick my tongue against hers, reveling in the way she's dripping for me.

Because she's bathing me in her excitement, and I've learned my beauty has a few weaknesses I'm not ashamed to explore:

I lick her fangs one at a time, not giving a single fuck if they cut me.

They're sharp and smooth, and I feel the small prick as Aya's pleasure turns into the most adorable tiny growl. This time, she's trying to buck me off from beneath and take control. I don't move, though. Instead, I savor her taste mixed with my blood, the dots only heightening Anaya's arousal, and I revel as her body rewards me with an all-body shiver.

"Goddess, Leo. I taste us." Wrong. It's not my blood that overpowers my senses—this passionate sweetness is simply her—and I repay her gift with aggressive desperation as I ravage her mouth. I take her lips as if this were my first and last taste; it's how I'll always kiss her.

I can't get enough of her. Never will.

Giving and taking, I memorize every inch of her mouth as my tongue slides across hers before nipping her top and bottom lip. And my queen doesn't fight her male for dominance, not because she has to submit to me, but because Aya wants to be mine.

Just like my possessiveness of her is only matched by her ownership of me.

"You're so fucking sweet, love."

"More. Give me more of you," she whimpers, body arching beneath mine. Then, there's the way Anaya spreads her lithe thighs a little wider and each time she gyrates—rubs her pink flesh over her mating mark—my thickness gives a harsh jerk. My pre-come mixes with her juices, creating the most intoxicating scent. "I need you, my male."

"Then take all of me." To provoke that beautiful creature that claimed me last night to come out and play, I pull back and give a sharp buck of my hips, roughly pushing my cock through her slick lips while lowering my full body weight on her. I'm covering Anaya from head to toe. My precious one feels so good—looks like perfection like this—a sentiment she shares as another rush of her wetness coats us and the bedsheets.

Anaya knows her place will always be beneath me, on top of me, but always with her legs spread and holes on display for her king. Just as I will never deny her. All that I am is hers, and when it's impossible to be present for me as duty takes precedence and our people have to come first, I will always have access to her.

Pussy. Ass. Mouth.

All three are mine, and I will never neglect her. Will always make her pleasure my priority.

"You're teasing me, love. That's not nice," Anaya hisses from between clenched teeth, flashing me her lovely little fangs. Her violet eyes are darker now, too. The pupils are blown wide and her nostrils flare a tiny bit, pulling my scent into her lungs. And the more she breathes me in, the harder her nipples pebble.

The more she arches up, offering her tits and pretty pink cunt.

"My apologies, precious one. Let me make it better." Bending my head, I take a stiff peak between my teeth and flick the tender flesh. Anaya is petite in stature, a breathing doll, but her curves are downright sinful. She's all childbearing hips and a perfectly round ass, but the perky, bigger-than-a-handful tits I'm cupping will forever be my downfall. They sit high on her chest and are littered with love bites from our mating, the perfect imprint of my teeth left behind, and I vow then that a single day will never pass without me tattooing myself on her flesh.

Be it by my seed.

Be it by my teeth.

Nipping the area just above her right nipple, I drag my teeth across her soft skin to her left breast and give it the same attention. I lick, tug, and suck on the tip before following its path down the underside where I leave another small bite. Harder. Then I love her a little lower, licking my precious one from her sternum to the area just above her mound and then back up again, cradling my hips at the juncture of her thighs.

Anaya's watching me with those hooded eyes, her lips parted and small, panting breaths escaping those supple lips. She follows my every move, taking in the way I grip myself and the pearl-like beads that pool at the tip before dripping onto her pussy.

Her hunger matches mine. It ripples through the bond, and it's tinged with a bit of frustration.

Take it, baby. Tell me what you need.

Slowly—reverently—I stroke myself against her clit. Just to let her feel me, the tip of my cock kissing her bundle of nerves before dipping lower until I'm notched at her entrance. I do this a few times, spreading my pre-come and her slickness while her hidden wildness makes an appearance.

She's stopped all movement as I press forward, feeding her two inches, and then I pull out.

Another stroke, just a little deeper, and her eyes narrow.

On the third pump of my hips, Anaya lifts her right hand and cups my chin, her fingernails digging in. That bite of pain makes me shiver, my lips curling up at the corners while Aya's lift, showing me her fangs.

"Something wrong, precious one?"

"Love me, my king." She's flushed, her cheeks rosy and mixed with a fine mist of sweat that covers her body from head to toe. "Ravish and break me before you baby me, Leo. I give you all of me, but please, just don't make me wait anymore."

"Good girl," I grit out before slamming into the hilt, not pausing to let her accommodate my size before pulling out and stroking deep once again. Immediately, my mate screams and her hips buck up to meet mine, all the while the hand on my face pets me, fingers caressing from jaw to lips. Her digits linger on my mouth for a few seconds on the third pass and I take two, sucking and nipping them while my hips pump in sharp, hard strokes.

Squelching noises fill the room, the sound obscene yet beautiful, and I close my eyes for a second to enjoy them. My cock drives deep and her back arches—completely lifting off the bed until nothing but her shoulders touch the mattress.

I follow the curves of her body with my hands, caressing and squeezing every inch of skin before slipping my arms beneath her back and gathering her close. Not a single inch of space between us, and if I'm holding her too tight, my queen doesn't complain. Instead, she wraps her shaking legs around my hips and mewls, both hands now embedded in my hair.

"Please don't stop," my girl hisses just before I kiss her, needing another taste of her lips. It's quick and rough; I devour and swallow every whimper as my tongue twines with hers. It's a little sloppy, and more than once her sharp fangs break my skin, but that only heightens our hunger.

I fuck her with a frenzy—almost as if I were experiencing a rut the way werewolves do—and punch my hips so hard we move up the bed. Her head meets the tufted headboard, one hand leaving my hair to brace against the ostentatious furniture, yet her hips don't stop moving.

For as much as need drives me, hers is right there with mine. She hums at the light taste of my blood, her lips tinged a light red, but it's the sudden gasp that breaks through the fog.

"Oh Goddess, Leo. *Oh!*"

I don't stop fucking her, sliding in and out of her wet heat. Loving the tightness, how her walls flutter and contract as she writhes in my arms, but I do take note of a few small changes.

Her violet eyes are almost black, and a small ring of the purple I love is left as the pupils expand. Then, there's the goosebumps rising across fevered skin; she's flushed and shivering, her toes digging into the small of my back.

And lastly, I find the imprint of my cock causing her stomach to bulge. Just a bit. Enough that I can make out just how deep I fuck her when the head sits a few inches below her belly button.

"Fuck, precious one," I grit out while lowering her back on the bed, yet keeping her pelvis tilted. One hip is in my grip while the other hand presses down on her lower abdomen so I can feel myself fuck her. "You're a gift. A sinful treasure."

"I'm so close. *Please.*" It's a whine. Another call to her male; I reply with a hard slam and bear down, feeding her every solid inch of my dick while stroking the tip of my thumb across her unhooded clit. At the moment, I feel more magic than man, the blood in my veins throbbing as I pulse against her walls.

And fuck me, she clenches so hard.

Anaya's mouth opens, but no words come out. Not a single sound, but her cunt works my length in response, matching my aura's vibrations with a velvety massage that pulls the first rope of come from me with ferocity.

I'm powerless against her. Owned by this tiny fae.

My balls are heavy.

My chest is so full of love for her.

"My beauty. My queen." This time I graze her bundle of nerves with the blunt edge of my fingernail before slamming in and out three times in rapid succession, fighting through my pleasure to take care of her. "Come for your king, love."

One soft touch, a single stroke, and Aya rewards immediately.

Those violet eyes shut and her head tips back as an orgasm slams into her, causing Anaya to scream for me. "Goddess, Leo. Oh, *fuck* me."

"Good girl. Milk my cock, sweetness." Another thing I've noticed about my female; she likes praise. Those two words set her off again—her hips rise in their limited space and gyrate, small little jerky movements before she locks up.

She doesn't move. Keeps me buried deep while her chest rises and falls rapidly.

Aya tightens, her walls molding around my length—gripping so tight I can't move—and a small growl rips from her. Her hunger isn't abated. If anything, it rises, and I begin to swell again.

I also don't pull out.

Instead, as her wings unfurl, I flip our positions, giving her one sharp smack across her right asscheek. She's impaled on my semi-hard cock while the bottom of her iridescent wings grazes my thighs.

Neither of us speak, our bodies moving to meet in small thrusts as the sound of skin meeting skin fills the room. We're a mess, slick with her release and mine; I inhale deeply and meld that scent with my DNA.

It's heady and sweet, the perfect mix of dark chocolate and strawberries with a hint of cream and spice. It's us. It's perfect.

"Motherfuck, my precious one. I could never live without you."

"And I love you." Her words are low, just a whisper while grinding down on me, rubbing her clit on my pelvis as her face lowers to mine. "You're my everything, Leo. My peace."

No sooner do those words leave her lips than she twitches, a series of involuntary movements, and holds her breath, falling forward onto my chest. Anaya's boneless in my hold as she comes again, her muscles spasming and the legs on either side of my hips lock up.

Her cries are no higher than a whisper yet powerful, and I wrap my arms around her while she rides each wave out. My still-hard cock slides in and out now. Lazily now. No rush.

I didn't come this time, but it doesn't matter.

Her pleasure is mine, and I'm a blessed man to call her mine.

Because she is. Every single part of her will forever belong to me.

Pressing a kiss to her sweaty temple, I smile against her sweat-slick skin. Breathe us in once again and thank the goddess for this gift because this right here, the feel of her in my arms, is heaven. Because nothing will ever matter more than her happiness, and if I must eradicate an entire kingdom to protect her, so mote it be.

I'll kill Silla when the time comes, too.

No one touches my queen.

My precious one.

CHAPTER 3
LEONARDO

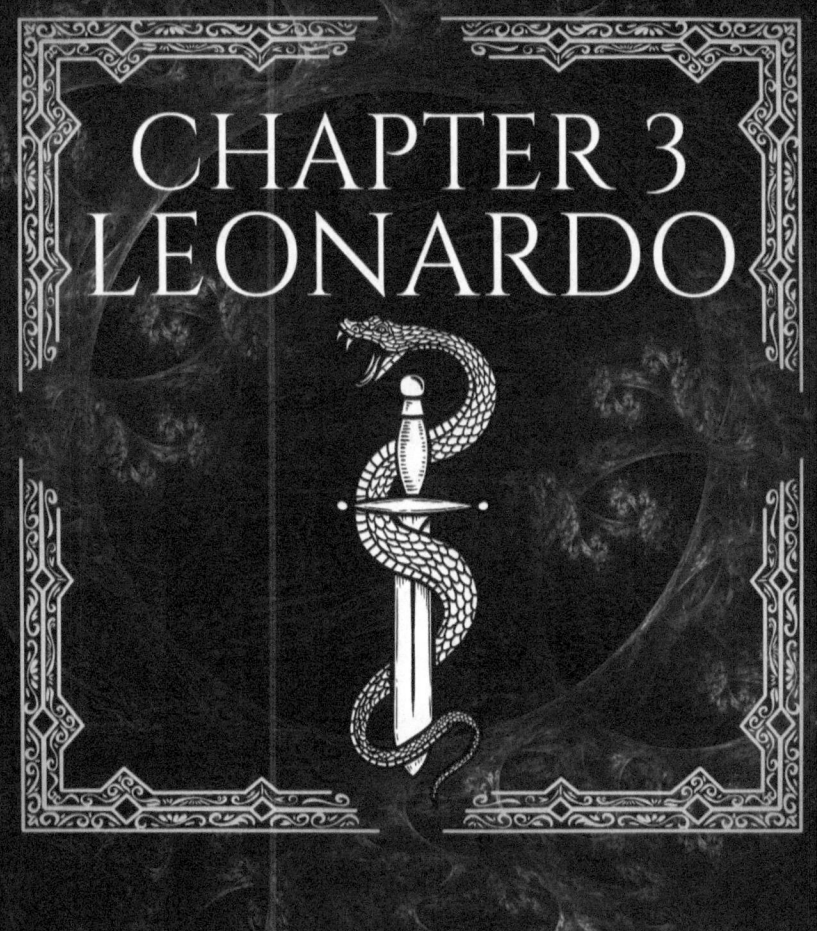

I t's a little past eight in the morning when my precious one rouses from her well-fucked-into sleep. She's curled up beside me, leg placed across my thighs while her long, golden hair fans out behind her. A few strands stick to the side of her neck and my arm, creating an interesting pattern that reminds me of lightning before it strikes the forest floor, and it's adorable.

Wild and untamed, Anaya is perfection like this to me.

Something about her being not put together—natural—makes me harder than steel, and my cock gives a not-so-subtle jerk against her flesh. It grazes the soft skin as it rises, each throb leaving behind a pearl-like drop until I'm standing straight and the sheet barely covering our lower halves tents.

That's what she opens her eyes to.

Her king's need. A hunger that only rises for her.

"Good morning, precious one," I say, my timbre deep, and she shivers, those doe eyes peering up at me while her lips part. A little owlish. Still so sleepy. Yet, she's aware, and the way her leg slides up until it grazes my hardness causes an instant change in me. From calm to near feral in an instant, and she's on her back before her next inhale, a low squeal slipping past that plump mouth.

Neither of us speak, the seconds ticking as I take her beauty in.

From her beautiful violet eyes to her dainty nose and then lower to those lips again. From how soft she looks—the way her skin reacts as I press her into the mattress, my full body weight over her. Then, there's how she parts her thighs to cradle my hips, still tender from our earlier mating while exhaling little gasps at the slightest shift of my dick against her slick flesh.

Anaya is always wet for me. Ready to receive her male, an automatic reaction that fills my chest with pride because this wonderous fae trusts me. Knows and accepts my love for her.

"Leo." That's all she says in the breathiest voice, her cheeks a warm pink that quickly spreads down across her chest. Her nipples are hard against my chest, and each rapid rise and fall of her chest rubs them across mine, gifting me small electrical pulses each time.

"My queen." Arching, she gyrates her hips and my thick shaft spreads those slick lips, bumping her clit with every stroke. I'm not going to fuck her. I know she's sore after taking me multiple times throughout the night, but I'll never leave my precious one wanting. "I love you, Anaya. The gods blessed me when they tied our souls. When they made you the beat of my heart."

"I—"

"Just feel me, sweetheart. Let me take care of you." I glide my mouth across hers before nipping her jaw. She gasps, but that quickly turns into a whimper as I press a little harder, rubbing her from tight hole to bundle of nerves and over again. And again.

I don't stop when she begs me to fuck her in a low, keening tone or when she embeds her nails into my back, breaking the skin as the first wave of pleasure rocks through her. Instead, I grip my cock with one hand while the other wraps around the front of her neck, just holding her in place.

I squeeze a few times while I pump myself, hard and fast strokes while the tip of my dick continues to rub her clit, kissing the trembling bundle as she comes for me and her eyes roll back, my hand tightening around her neck and my cock until she's covered in me.

Rope after rope of come lands across her cunt—her mound and clit—the clenching entrance soaked in our combined release. Soaked and slick and a pretty pink as it spreads and dribbles down to the sheets below.

I watch each drop as it slides, some lingering on her labia before following the path between her asscheeks and then to the bedding. And while I enjoy the view, I feel Anaya's eyes on me.

Love the way my skin heats under her stare.

How my cock gives another jerk, already semi-hard for her as a few more drops of my spend fall on her skin.

My girl exhales roughly then, pulling my attention to her face where I find those lips curled in a devious grin. She's also flushed and a bit sweaty, her sweet scent heady. "You made a mess, King Moore."

"Not going to deny it." I return her amusement with a smirk of my own while sliding the tip of my dick over our combined release. "It makes for a pretty picture, too."

"Such a naughty monarch."

"A completely feral deviant for you. Only ever you."

Anaya's face softens at that, her earlier reaction coming to the forefront. Through our bond, I felt her emotions: from jealousy to anger and then worry. There was also a touch of sadness that hovered around the edges of every other emotion, her body throbbing from head to toe because of her memories.

"Are you ready to talk, Aya? Tell me what happened earlier."

She purses her lips but nods. "Yes, but I want to do it with Gabriella and Theodore present. This could affect us all...I think it ties everyone."

"All of us?"

"Every kingdom."

"Okay." Lifting myself from her warmth after a final kiss, I climb off the bed before dragging her to the edge and then tossing Aya's squealing body over my shoulder. My hand immediately goes to her ass, squeezing and kneading as I march us to the en-suite bath. We're going to see my family as she asked, and I *will* fix whatever upset her earlier, but first I want to clean her up and then dirty her before lathering my female a second time.

"You're a caveman. So brutish." She's giggling as I place her on her feet, turning her to face the shower wall furthest away from the rainfall water feature. Steam billows around us, the water lapping against my skin. "We're supposed to be cleaning up, then talk..."

"And we will. I never want to feel like that again—you being anything but happy and content is unacceptable to me, my precious one." My whispered words against the shell of her ear have the desired effect, and she melts back into me, not an inch of space between us. "But I need you to spread them first, sweetheart. I haven't had my breakfast yet."

A devious distraction, I admit, but just like I'll destroy anything that harms her, the compulsion to reassure Anaya is just as strong. That taste of jealousy from earlier still lingers on my tongue, so tiny it's barely discernible, and that much is intolerable to me.

As her mate, I take care of her and no one else.

I love her.

I breathe for her.

"Like this, my king?" she asks, voice coy. See the corner of her lips quirking a bit.

"Yes." It's bit out, my nostrils flaring as the scent of her arousal rises. Aya moans and pushes back against me as I slide two fingers over her clit before slipping them inside her already clenching hole. "And I'll reward you for your trust, my love. First with my tongue, and then cock, before spilling your enemy's blood at your feet. So more it be."

"It's good to see you, Aya. How are you feeling?" Gabriella asks from her perch on Theodore's lap an hour later, her grin cheeky while her husband gently runs his fingers through her red hair. He's stroking the long strands slowly, mesmerized by the feel of them, while my sister emits a low purr and rubs the back of her head against his shoulder and his answering rumble reverberates throughout these dark walls.

Neither are embarrassed by the act, and those inside the vampiric throne room do not look their way. Instead, they bow before exiting, firmly closing the ornate doors as we stop in front of the dais where an oversized, blood-red tufted chair made of the darkest ebony and crushed bones stands proud.

The throne is macabre, a symbol of power and domination just like the rest of the room.

Moreover, as you step inside the vampiric royal chambers, the heavy scent of ancient blood greets you, mingling with a touch of sweetness that I recognize as kin.

Isabella, of jasmines. Gabriella, of cherries.

Yet they carry a small ribbon of lavender in their scent markers that represent our familial bond—my mother's favorite scent—that only we can detect. I carry that note, too. It's a precaution our parents put into place the day of our christening, making sure that no matter where we are in the world, we can always find our way to each other.

No one can break these ties. We can never be truly lost.

My nose twitches then as another fragrance infiltrates my senses, and my precious one has the same reaction: incense. It burns inside of ornate censers while solid gold sconces and a large, crystal chandelier bathe the room in dimmed crimson light. The glow bounces off the all-black walls and the thick, red velvet drapes that trail from the room's high ceilings to the polished obsidian floors.

This room is heavy with the lingering screams of death.

This room has witnessed the truest love.

This room is marked by sigils belonging to the God of Death in honor of his children: the vampire king and his bride.

My brother-in-law. My sister.

"Good to see you, Gabby."

"Hello to you, too, Sister," Anaya and I answer in unison, my beauty giving me a small jab with her elbow, and I find the action quite adorable. Speaks of the ease she has to joke or correct me—be open and sassy with me—and the smile on my face can't be missed because of it. And while Gabriella snorts at our behavior, her mate simply raises a brow that's quickly followed by a nod of understanding.

The men mated to my sisters love them beyond all reason.

Each king is brutal and unapologetic in their blood thirst when crossed, but for their mates, they kneel. Defer and ask—honor Isabella and Gabriella's wishes—and now more than ever, I understand both sides of their characters.

Because I am both.

A killer.

Anaya's willing servant.

"Get used to it, King Moore. You've been moved to the end of the line." Gabby's hiss is playful, and it pulls a giggle from the woman beside me, my female's shoulders shaking in amusement. We watch her laugh. Even the stoic vampire king softens a bit, and I'm pleased by how they've accepted her. As if reading my thoughts, my sister taps her heart. "By blood and pact."

"We are one." We answer in unison, and I'm surprised when Anaya's voice intermingles with mine and Theodore's.

"What?" she asks, blushing at the intense way I turn my face and watch her. My miracle fae.

"How did you know about—?"

"Gabriella and Isabella taught me the day after I arrived here. We were on FaceTime..." my girl pauses for a moment, brows furrowed "...that's what they called it."

"You're right. It is called FaceTime." When she says things like that, pure confusion on her face, I'm reminded once again of how sheltered she grew up. How her father abused and kept her hidden— forced her to live under a tyranny that protected men and subjugated fae women. Bending toward her, I place my kiss against her temple. "And I should've taught you our vow, my female. That promise will hold deeper meaning between us."

"How so?" she whispers as I lay another small peck on her fragrant skin, dragging my lips down to her cheek. "I don't—"

"Because every part of me is now a part of you, love. My heart. My blood. My very soul." My voice is low, but the gravelly timbre sweeps across her and she moves closer, shivering a bit. "I'm irrevocably tied to you until my last dying breath, Anaya, and even then, I'll still be yours."

"Mine." One word, but it holds so much emotion.

My response is quick, and I grasp the back of her neck while turning her face up to mine. Those violet eyes are happy, her lips curling a bit—lips that I now hover against. "In this life and every single one that follows, I will be *yours*."

"As I belong to you."

I don't care about the other two witnessing our moment— nothing and no one could stop me from fully tasting her lips. I kiss her again. Slowly and reverently, taking and giving while pouring every bit of my feelings for her into every sweep of my tongue or nibble to her bottom lip, then the top one.

I hold her to me and don't stop devouring that sinful mouth until she's breathless, and only then do I pull back and lay a tiny peck on the tip of her nose before giving our family my attention once more.

What I find doesn't surprise me.

One is looking at me with complete happiness, and the other's attention is solely on the near-giggling vampire witch on his lap.

"When are we having the bonding ceremony?" Gabriella asks the second Aya stops blushing. For a second, she forgot our audience, and I'm proud of it. Revel in the way I affect my tiny fae queen. "It's been so long since our people have rejoiced in a royal union."

As soon as the words leave Gabby, she looks at me and all noises cease. For that secular moment, we're back to that day—the familial connections we share thrums with sadness—and bits of the last horror-filled moments of our parents' lives flash before my eyes. I'm sure she's remembering, too, and while there will always be sadness and loss, we're not alone anymore.

Now, as Anaya slips her hand into mine, there's comfort and the promise of new memories that will begin overriding—erasing the last moments with our parents. I'm reminded of the happier times in my childhood and with it comes the desire to give our future offspring the same kind of love and safety we were raised on.

From Mom cleansing our home with sage and herbs or the times she baked our favorite desserts in the kitchen. To Father teaching us our first spells, and when things went wrong, which they do for all new witches, he'd repair what we broke after calming his offspring with a hug. His magical tethers would wrap around us while he explained and taught with all the patience in the world.

Isabella burned his desk.

Gabriella shattered an ancient Wiccan mortar that belonged to our first ruler.

I made our paternal grandfather's grimoire disappear, and to this day, I still don't know where it vanished.

Not once did he get angry. Instead, Father found our magical *mishaps* amusing.

"Mistakes create character, Leo. It will humble you, and you three will need that. My offspring will one day rule this world, and being perfect leads to egotistical tyranny and selfish leaders—I want

you to mess up. To burn things, my son, because one day those same frustrating moments will help you lead with mindfulness and empathy.

"Soon, Sister, but first—"

"Like the next new moon, soon?"

"I'll let you know once we decide. We actually—"

"You haven't discussed it yet? What are you waiting—"

"Gabriella, Anaya needs to speak with everyone." That stops my sister from asking any more questions as both vampires sit up straighter, their blood-red eyes on my mate. They don't speak. Instead, they tilt their heads simultaneously while I move my eyes back to their favorite place: on her. "Tell us, sweetheart. What upset you earlier, Anaya?"

CHAPTER 4

Anaya

"*What upset you earlier, Anaya?*" Leo's question hangs in the air as two cell phones go off at the same time, his and mine, but before I can respond, another one pings, and the vampire king merely raises a brow. His eyes flick to his mate, their exchanged looks knowing, as another text comes in within seconds of the first—four in total before Theo blindly reaches for the device set atop a modern side table that I'd missed before.

The design is simple yet unique, and I can't help but smile at something I'm more than positive Gabriella chose. Its concept makes it appear as if blood drips from the round tabletop, thick beads of red frozen in time, while the legs complete the look in the same manner. There's a fluidity to the table—this suspended-in-time moment of a gory ending—while the touch of gold in the filigree design at the bottom of each leg gives it a touch of glamour.

Unique, it sits beside the royal couple with no other purpose than to hold their mobiles.

She's always had a taste for the macabre, precious one. It's always been her quirk. Leo's voice inside my head causes me to let out a small gasp while his sister takes the offered device from her mate, ignoring us. And while my reaction should embarrass me, it doesn't. I would honestly live through a thousand years of humiliation for this brief moment of bliss. It's the sweetest caress across my every processor, a stroke down my nerve endings, and a complete contrast to the painful manipulations I'd been raised by.

His voice in my head is full of love, not spite.

Not hate, but honest respect. Appreciation.

Not just hers, my king. I've seen your collection of medieval weapons. My lips quirk at his faux indignant expression, but I'm not buying it. More so when his jaw ticks and eyes crinkle a bit from holding back a laugh. *Or are you going to deny the time you've spent organizing, maintaining, and cataloging each item?*

"I'm guilty, Anaya. Won't deny it." Leonardo tilts his head a bit, and I'm lit up from within at the sudden heat in his blue eyes. They give me a slow perusal, from head to toe, before ending the flirtatious move with a not-innocent shrug. *I've lived a hundred years without you and spent every single one of those minutes occupying my time—collecting things—to ease the loneliness. And when I wasn't taking care of my people or researching ways to kill your father, I hoarded treasures. I did everything in my power to make those endless seconds pass because giving another woman what is solely yours was a crime I would never commit.*

A throat clears, pulling our attention toward the throne where we find the two vampires watching us. One has a happy expression and the other, a stony one, the latter, which I've come to realize in my time at the vampiric kingdom, their king's default. He's also still holding up the cell phone, which his mate has made no move to take.

Instead, the vampire queen simply laughs. "It's Isa. We need to video call her."

"Have you spoken—" Leo begins, but she snorts, cutting him off. The sound is so childlike, innocent, and the complete opposite of the powerful witch/vampire sitting atop her throne and mate's thigh.

"Yes. They'll be here later this evening."

"What did she see?"

"The same thing your mate has come to realize, little brother," Isabella's voice cuts through, and my male's head snaps in my direction to find me holding up my mobile with a connected call. Both Isa and Xadiel are in the camera shot, but where the vampire king is stoic, the alpha wolf grins. He gives us a nod but remains silent, his luna securely on his lap.

The two are more alike than they think. When it comes to their mates, they need constant contact and protect them viciously.

Just like Leo with me. He killed my brother for me.

"Are you angry with me, Anaya?" Leo asks after our last shower of the night. I'd been wrapped up in his embrace wearing nothing but a towel, my head tucked beneath his chin, knees weak after coming on his tongue that final round. "I'm sorry it came to that; I'd never want to cause you pain, but Ruben was a threat, one I couldn't allow to live after what he did."

"I'm not mad, my love." And it's the truth. There's no mourning or pain at the knowledge that the man I grew up believing to be my kin is now dead. "Ruben was evil, Leo. His ending was just deserved."

"You grew up with him."

"He also made my life miserable." Tipping my head back, I meet his soft blue eyes and smile. "Is it wrong that all I feel is relief? Utter and brilliant relief at knowing he will never hurt anyone again?"

"Not at all. You are entitled to every emotion, sweetheart." Bending a bit at the waist, he brings our faces—mouths—to hover. To slide back and forth against the other's lips as I breathe in his every exhale. "You survived. You gave every bit of who you are to take care

of your people, your mother, while your father tore you down. I'm proud of you, Anaya."

I've never had someone outside of my mother see me. Care so much about me.

A knot forms in my throat and a small sob slips, my chest feeling lighter than it has in years. Sometimes you don't realize how starved for love you are until someone selflessly envelops you in warmth and affection.

"Thank you."

"No tears, baby. Please." With gentle hands, he cups my face and wipes them away with his thumbs. "Nothing cuts me more than this. All I want is your happiness and to give you back everything you've lost."

The way he words it makes me pause, and my brows furrow; I feel as if there's a deeper meaning to that declaration. "What do you—"

"There's so much I still need to explain, should've told about already, but the mating lust hasn't released me yet. For that conversation, I need my faculties sharp, Anaya. Can you wait until tomorrow morning so I don't butcher this?"

"Yes."

"Thank you."

Understanding him isn't difficult, especially after my moment of weakness—the raw emotions that come from finding your mate and finally marking them differ vastly. There's lust, so much love through the fully formed ties that connect us, and interwoven within each emotion is a possessiveness that's all-consuming.

The moment my fangs sunk into his cock, I experienced a flash of heat and hunger that overwhelmed me. It controlled me as I licked every inch of my king before I rode him and then presented my body for his free use.

I gave myself to him. All of me. And he loved me so thoroughly that the earlier bout of jealousy and those memories slipped away into a dark corner of my mind—until now.

"Her scent, Leo. That's what we missed," Isabella and I say in unison, causing the others to let out a low growl or hiss. Especially the man beside me; his chest rumbles while strong arms encircle my waist, pulling me back flush against a hard chest. He almost causes me to drop the phone and takes notice right away, slipping the device from my hand and tossing it to Theodore.

The vampire, whose red eyes are now narrowed, catches it and then swipes a finger over the screen. There's something he searches for, and when he finds it and taps on the glass again, it begins to make a weird sound. It rattles and something clangs, but then I realize it's the whir of a mechanical pulley system moving. To the left of us, there's a wall covered by ruby-red drapes that begins to part, revealing a large screen underneath.

Leo's other sister and her mate greet the four of us, and I'm confused for a second until Gabriella gives a small, indulgent clap. Her smile is wide. "I told you this would be perfect in here, Theo. A few modern touches here and there wouldn't diminish—"

"You are right as always, pretty girl." Theodore kisses the side of her head, his lips moving but we can't hear the rest of what he says. All we see is *her* reaction, and it isn't innocent. Gabriella's eyes turn a darker, richer shade of red while she fights to control her fangs from dropping. They still peak out. Just the very tips. There's also a not-so-subtle shiver, and when I look back at Isabella on the screen, the werewolf luna simply winks at me and mouths, *hi.*

So it's a giant phone screen on the wall? Behind me, Leo chuckles, a little of his protective anger dissipating. "You heard me?"

I did, and you're bloody adorable, Anaya. Nothing is more precious in my world than you.

Nothing?

You are my everything. Then I'm given a quick nuzzle to my cheek before he stands to his full height, my body securely against his. He doesn't so much as let me take a step forward and I'm okay with it, love how open this family is with affection between mates.

In the fae kingdom, that's an abhorrent behavior unless it's just to fuck.

As sexual creatures, men can take carnal pleasure without recrimination—we're not prudish in the least—but that's where it ends. Faes being insatiable lovers is one thing, taking multiple partners—male and female is praised—but not for love. To satiate, not to honor and cherish.

There are no kisses in public or open displays of affection for your mate. Even the act of holding hands for too long is seen as whorish of the woman. You are tempting the male and bringing shame to your home. My father's rules keep men in charge. They hold all positions of power, while the women are there to serve, pleasure, and take care of the home.

To raise the next generation of warriors or maids.

Because that's what all women—outside of Silla—were to him and Ruben.

Maids. Submissive servants.

It's a decree given to me the day I turned thirteen summers, and I was reminded of every birthday after. My mother was given the task up until her death, and then my father took over. This time, though, with the promise of my upcoming nuptials to his favored general.

When in public, a woman's place is three steps behind her husband.

You look at no one but him or the ground.

Do not speak out of turn.

He is the head of the house, and no one comes before him.

His word is law, and you must obey. Never question his decisions.

You will remain untouched until the day of your wedding.

"Explain, precious one." Leo turns me toward him and then cups my face, tilting it until I'm looking into those beautiful blue eyes. "I don't understand what you mean by scent. Who are we talking about?"

"Chiara Rossi."

Behind me, there are two hisses at the name, sharp and loud, and two large guards step into the room. The men bend at the waist, their necks bared in a gesture of respect for all in the room, and they nod at each of us.

"Your Majesties," Tero greets the room, slipping between the vampire guards. His body is half-shifted. From the waist down, the large albino body is coiled to strike the nonexistent threat inside the room. "We are at your service."

"I'll need your help locating two witches." It's not Theodore who speaks, but Leo, his voice reverberating throughout the room. Tinged with anger. Hatred. "Chiara and Lena were last seen in Paris after running from my coven. Both women seem to have gone underground; they're the last remaining Rossi clan members."

I catch on to the emphasis he put on the word *last*.

The day I left the Wiccan kingdom, Leo had his suspicions. Neither of us trusted those women, the way they showed up and claimed their leader was missing while both Ruben and Brice miraculously escaped. Coincidences don't exist, but precisely executed opportunities do.

You wait for the right time. You move and never apologize for the manipulation.

I learned that from my father. From years of watching him create celebrations in his name without ever dirtying his hands, and yet, if you heard the man speak on his accomplishments, you'd think otherwise.

Roi de cons. He was the king of idiots.

"Why were they on the property, Leo? That family cannot be—"

"Christopher is dead," Isabella cuts Gabriella off, and my male confirms with a nod. "Those two murdered him, but they had help. Vampires, at that."

"How many, Isa?" Theodore's voice thunders, striking fear into his subjects, and the two guards drop to their knees while Tero lowers his head. "More than those already in my custody?"

"Get a head count of all military personnel. You'll have your answer."

"I'll get right on that, my king. I'm confident I'll sniff the Rossis out and escort them here within a few days, but first, I'll get that count for you," Tero says, dragging the letter *S* each time. Theo nods at him and all three of his men begin to exit the room, but the constrictor pauses beside us. "Give me an hour and I'll be ready to leave. I'll have an accurate count and names of the missing by then."

Leo inclines his head. "I'll wait for you on the training field, and Augusto will be expecting you back home so you can pick up the lingering traces of their scents. The cabin they used has been untouched since they ran."

"As you wish." Flicking his eyes toward me, the serpentine shifter gives me a gentle smile. "Congratulations, young one. May your mating be blessed and happy all the days of your life."

"Thank you, Mr. Tero." With another bow, this time to both Leonardo and me, he heads out and begins giving orders to the two accompanying him. And once their voices become low and their footsteps near nonexistent, Isabella clears her throat.

"He's right, you know." All heads turn in Isabella's direction, yet her eyes are on me. So much knowledge in that stare, but the weight of it sets off alarm bells. "You've been deceived all your life, Anaya. The truth has always been within reach, and nothing is stopping you this time from claiming what's yours by birthright. One of two surviving héritière."

"What about Silla and Brice? Will they be a problem?"

"Yes, but not in the way you think. Those who oppose you will die, but it's the journey that will cost you. The universe never forgets, and the price owed will be claimed." Fear settles into the pit of my stomach at Isabella's warning, churning and reminding me of everything I've lived through, and yet the moment my mate places his hand on the small of my back, I'm settled. *I'm no longer alone. Never again.* "Are you ready for it? To confront the truth?"

Letting out a shaky breath, I nod. "I am."

"Then it's time you two sit down and talk, my sister of the heart. Share your dreams, while I discuss a few things with Gabriella and Theodore before we arrive."

CHAPTER 5
LEONARDO

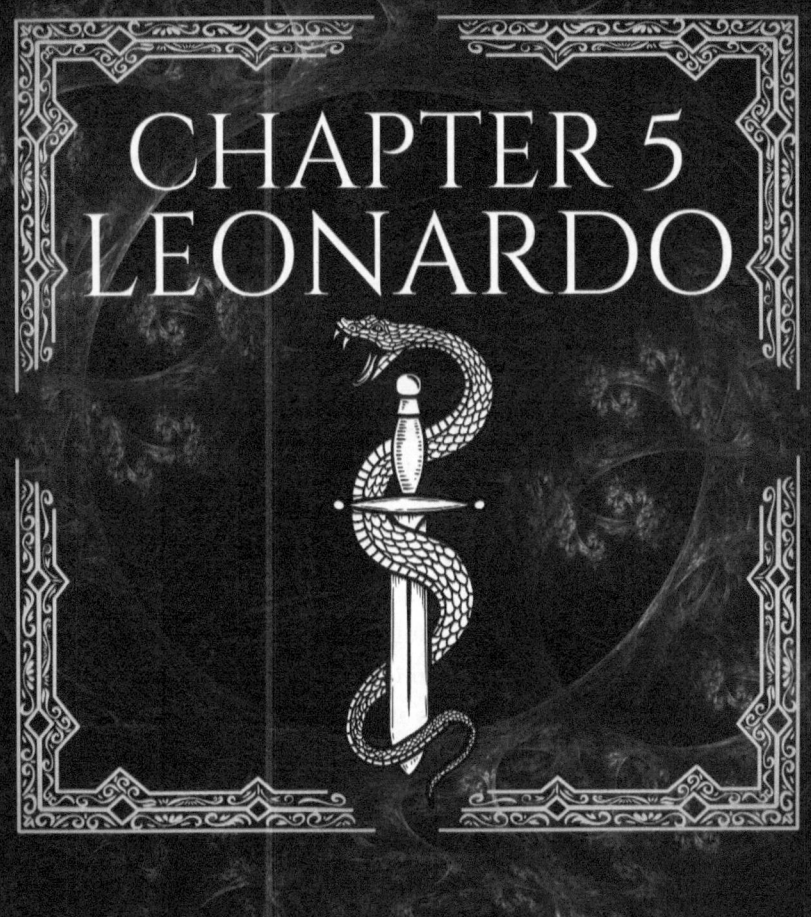

I sabella speaks to Anaya, but the message is meant for me.

There's a hint of warning in her words, a bit of reproach, and it's confirmed a few seconds later when my sister flicks her eyes in my direction, a sad expression on her face. She's seen something—maybe my precious one's reaction to my news—and while every part of me wants to protect Anaya from the potential pain, this time I can't.

She deserves to know:

About her father.

About the man she grew up believing to be her brother.

And lastly, her mother.

"Please excuse us. We'll be retiring to our room, and I ask that we're not disturbed."

"Of course, Leo. Take all the time you need." Theodore's deep voice startles Anaya and she jumps a bit, her hands trembling lightly. "I'll be at the training grounds when you meet with Tero. No rush on that either."

"I appreciate that."

"A few matters do need our immediate attention before Tero leaves, though. *They* will not pass this evening without judgment." The sinister inflection of his voice belies a hidden message. *Passing judgment* is meant to soften the hidden decree for blood and his brand of justice, Theo's ruby red stare displaying his hunger for vengeance, and while my girl doesn't take full notice of the change—I do.

Theodore Astor has always been a ruthless king, make no mistake about that, and yet his softened expression is on my mate. Not an ounce of anger or the need to defend himself is found in him. Instead, the vampire king gives me an understanding look while mouthing *go*.

Anaya's not afraid of him but lost in her thoughts.

Yet there's protectiveness there. A sense of worry. A reaction that reminds me of how his entire being transformed when he took a bullet meant to kill Isabella. It bounced off him leaving no mark behind, but the gesture spoke loudly to every being present.

She is—we are all—family. There's a brotherly bond that links us.

And fuck me if that—the way they all watch out for Aya— doesn't bring me peace. Because if anything, Goddess forbid, were to ever happen to me, they'd watch out for her. My little mate would never be alone ever again.

"Come, Anaya." Nothing. She doesn't move. My female's lost in her head and I step closer, the hand at her back clutching her soft dress as I turn my head to fully watch my female.

An open book, Aya's open emotions fly across her face. They switch from fear to hope and then to a bit of trepidation, while through the bond, I get her urge to withdraw into herself and that's unacceptable to me.

What's wrong, my love? I speak through our mental link, but she shakes her head instead of responding. Her posture is a little tense, and the more I take her in, I notice the same behaviors she exuded the day we met.

Timid.

Lost.

Needy.

The last one hits me square in the gut, and I tuck Anaya's small body against my own. The palpable response is instantaneous. That lithe little body sags against me as the arm at her back wraps around her waist, her chest exhaling roughly.

"What do you need, precious one?"

"A moment," she says, her voice so low no one else can hear.

"Come with me." Giving her side a quick squeeze, I step back and then tap the back of her elbow before extending the same hand. My digits wiggle a bit, the invitation there, and my queen doesn't disappoint as a moment later, her delicate fingers slip into mine. Through our mating connection, I sense her need to feel grounded. To soothe her fragile nerves. I return her trust by tugging us out of the room.

Neither of us speak as the doors close behind us and the murmur of our family speaking becomes fainter. Each step toward her quarters in the castle—the room where we completed our mating—is heavily weighted by her nerves and my growing need to kill her demons.

The memories attached to her family and the fae kingdom will always haunt her; she lived so much of her life shackled by their ugliness, by the lies and subjugation, and lastly, by the way King Larue cruelly removed her mother and then made her believe the fae queen had passed. Moreover, I know this will bring her both joy and pain, but it's the latter that makes me pause.

Being the cause of a single tear is unacceptable. Hurts.

"Do you trust me?" A whisper from Anaya pulls me from my thoughts, but to me, it's as if she's shouted it from the rooftops. Four words, and they taste bitter. It causes me to pause and take a deep breath, but my reaction is beyond me. Can't stop myself. "Leo? What's going…oh!"

Her back meets the wall and my hands are on her thighs, lifting her so we're face to face. So those violet eyes can see my every emotion—the truth in my words. Sweet heat greets the head of my semi-hard cock through a thin layer of clothing, my trousers doing little to hide how ready for me she is.

Her dress is bunched up, and her bare pussy sits directly over my thickness; I want to rip my pants off and empale her on her throne. *Not now, but after. We have the rest of our lives.*

I made sure to get rid of every pair of panties inside her room on the property. There will never be a single stitch of clothing keeping her from me, and that's a law I will never bend or break. Back home, I'd given my queen time to adjust to us—to my touch and hunger— but that ended the moment she marked my cock with her tiny fae fangs.

She is mine. I am hers. End of.

Because the way I want her isn't in question, just as her cunt drips for me—the sweet slick staining my trousers—but this isn't the time to act on it. Right now, my female needs her mate to explain, and then help her pick up the pieces of her shattered heart because what they've done will hurt.

"I'm going to need you to listen to me, my love. Really listen to me." She knows I'm not expecting a verbal answer and merely gives me a nod of acknowledgment. *Good little fae.* "If there's anyone in this life that I trust, it's you. *You,* Anaya, are my heart. *You* are my reason for living and my partner in crime. No one will guard me as you do, just as I will lay down my life to protect yours. You, Anaya, are the answer to every question I've ever had, and I know you'd never betray me. Your beautiful soul wouldn't let you."

"Then why are you hiding something from me?" While her voice is timid, I'm proud of the determination I see in her eyes. Unwavering. "Why did Isabella say there are two heirs if Ruben is dead?"

With my hips pinning her against the wall, I lift my hands to her face and cup a cheek in each. My smile is small, my forehead lying on hers. "Because Ruben was never next in line, Anaya."

"What?" A question, but there isn't much emotion in her inflection. If anything, she's flat. As if she were merely speaking about the weather. "How can that be?"

"Explain or confirm?"

"Both."

"Fair enough, but let's do so in our room." Pushing us off the wall, I walk up the stairs, not stopping until we're at the foot of the large unmade bed. Our scent lingers all over the room, her come—a natural saccharine note—pulls a deep rumble from inside my chest. It travels through her, my beautiful mate biting her lips as she fights the urge to roll her hips against my hard cock.

It takes all of my strength to not move, but then I feel Anaya give a minuscule grind—the tiniest gyration of her hips—earning a sharp hiss from me. For me to bare my teeth before I toss her atop the strewn sheets and follow her giggling body down.

That laugh helps break the tension, and Anaya doesn't fight me when I situate us, my back against the headboard while she sits nestled between my thighs. My arms wrap around her petite frame, my chin on her head. "Better, precious one?"

"Yes." For a few seconds, we stay quiet. We just sit and be, and I've never in my life felt so at ease in another person's presence. There's no need to fill the silence with mundane chatter—not that we don't talk a lot, but it's not necessary either. Sometimes, in moments like this, when nothing is said, deeper connections are built. We find peace in each other. We're more than okay to let the bond connecting us thrum with pleasurable electricity.

We're conduits for this living, breathing pulse; born to walk this life together.

"Let me start this with a question, Anaya." Her head bobs in acceptance of my statement. "Did you already suspect that Ruben wasn't your mother's son? That Larue passed him off as Amelia's after he killed the woman who birthed the sniveling weakling trying to pass off as the next fae king."

From my vantage point, I watch Anaya exhale roughly and then pout her lips. "To be honest…no, I'm not surprised. Not at all—"

"There's a *but* in there."

"Because a part of me always questioned how differently Ruben and I were raised. Why he had everything, while I was forced to comply and live in fear? Not for me, but for my mother's sake. Every part of me wanted to rebel against the *king's* orders…" she spit out the word with disdain "…but I knew that if I did, he'd hurt her. Both of them would. He promised me as much."

"I'm sorry, precious one. We waited too long to deal with him and the fake prince."

"Not your fault." Tilting her head back, Anaya looks up at me, and those violet eyes hold so much regret. So much pain. "I wasn't affected like others in our kingdom, Leo, and that's something I wondered about every day. Asked myself why he hated my mother and me so much."

"He was a sick fuck, Anaya. All he cared about was power."

Roi de cons. I lift my left brow at that in question, and a small giggle slips out of her. Such an innocent sound. "He was the king of idiots, my male. A man with no moral compass who thrived under the lies he created for self-importance and to reinforce the narrative that a woman can't lead."

"That's bullshit." Anger and disgust tinge my tone.

"I know."

"Why didn't they know about your powers, Anaya?" Since meeting my little fae, I've kept heavy talks to a minimum to not overwhelm her. I've loved her and shown her she can trust me without asking for anything in return, but no more. Now we're going to confront everything together, fight for her people together because she is the rightful queen.

We'll rule both kingdoms as one. I'll never ask her to give up her birthright, just as I'm not going to control her; my female only kneels for her king in the bedroom, as I will for her. As leaders, we're equals, and her ideas and opinions are just as important as mine.

"Because all I had was my mother, Leo."

"I know that, but what does it have to do—"

"She begged me to never show them my ability. No matter what, I wasn't to interfere and heal her, but I was stubborn and didn't listen. The last time I did, he'd..."

"What did that bastard do, Anaya?"

"He had bled her for black practices after a *punishment*." She takes in a deep inhale, giving herself a moment to gather her thoughts. "At the time, I didn't know Father used her magic—the very ties that flow through her veins—to control those who opposed him. You see, the fae are connected through blood to their monarchy, and my mother's essence was the key to his rise. Because of her, they felt the sacred bond within him. That's why each member of our kingdom answered the call. Why they kneeled for the man wearing a golden crown—their very being demanded it—and I'd grown up thinking it was normal. That he was our rightful leader."

"But it changed? How did you figure it out?"

"Because walls are thin, and I listened. I made it my job to care for Maman when he'd taken so much she couldn't walk right after. I also visited the library quite a bit behind the guise of polishing my lessons on royal etiquette. All lies, but I began to put things together, and later, having her confirm things further cemented my perception." She's pensive again, as if remembering. Reliving. "Father was someone untrustworthy. *He* was wrong for our people."

"Why didn't your mother reclaim her throne? Leave with you?" That earns me a displeased tug through our bond; a literal yank of the symbolic chain that binds our souls, making me grunt and then

chuckle. Our connection is a wondrous thing. From the very beginning, it's demolished everything I knew about mates—defies rationality—and I find myself living for each little discovery we make
along the way. "Be nice, precious one. I'm just asking a question
while trying to jog your memory. No malice intent."

"Why?"

"Because of something Ruben said. Need to verify it."

"I'm going to need more than that." Once more, she doesn't play
nice. Instead, Anaya gives me another sharp pull, and it's not so
much that she's annoyed this time, but more so because she can. My
earlier reaction amused her, even though the subject matter at hand
was difficult.

"Anaya." Voice a near growl. Playful, yet hungry.

"Or what?" *The little tease.*

She's bratty. A bit sassy.

And I motherfucking love her all the more for trying to lighten
the heavy discussion. Not for herself, but because she feels what I do
—my worry and trepidation—and is trying to ease me. Selfless, even
if it hurts her. *The same way she took care of Amelia all those years.*

Exhaling roughly, I press my lips to the crown of her head and
simply breathe her in. Stay that way as I tighten my hold on her.
"Right now, we're going to finish this conversation, and then I'm
going to meet with Tero and Theodore. But make no mistake, Anaya.
I'm going to tally each offense, starting with the way you reacted
earlier in bed, and make you repent on your knees and then on your
back later. Not today, though. Today, I'll baby you."

A shiver runs through her at the same time her natural scent
spikes—that strawberries-and-cream decadence—just enough to let
me know I affect her. Unlike shifters who feel the pull through scent,
Wiccans see the physical manifestation like plumes of smoke. Not
large, but rather a mist that rises from her skin, more so after mates
vow themselves to each other.

Father explained this would happen during one of our many
talks.

You'll see her colors, my son. They'll call out and surround you like an early morning mist, providing cover while guiding your way to her. The Gods will never hide your female from you.

"Today, I'll soothe you and give your heart the refuge it needs, but come daylight, I'm going to fuck you. I'll reassure the little fae who marked my cock, whose fangs left behind the most beautiful mating imprint, that I am hers. That she will always own me."

CHAPTER 6

Anaya

His promise settles my being.

Maybe it's the emotion behind each syllable or the way he stares at me, sees me, that mends together the shattered pieces left behind by my family. Even now, knowing that my father and brother are dead—that they'll never physically hurt me again—I'm reminded of every snide word or sting of their hands. That they'd rather me be dead than happy with my true mate.

I could've missed out on this had they forced me to accept Brice.

But then, there's Leonardo's touch.

How one single caress from a fingertip or the way he cages me in brings me to life. My back is currently to his front while his exhales give way to small kisses between each whispered vow of *I'm here.*

He's warm and open and his *worry* for me is touching. Because I've gone through life yearning—to know I'm the center of someone's universe—and it's something I could never live without again.

I'm spoiled by his care. Grounded by his presence. And if there's one thing I've learned about my male and admire him for, it's that his love language is overwhelming.

Honest. Pure. Devotion.

This time, the yank I give our bond is playful, a coquettish response from a woman so enamored with her mate. So thankful. I can't explain how I'm doing it, physically manipulating the bond, but I'm enjoying the effect it has on him.

I see it and *feel* it.

His amusement and desire to claim me all over again, but he doesn't. *Not today.*

Another way I respect him is how he puts my needs above his own. His cock is hard and throbbing, each pulse against my fabric-covered lower back sending ripples of pleasurable shocks to my system—I feel his need calling to me through the bond—but Leo holds back.

He rejects his instinct, the debased hunger, and continues to soothe me.

Tilting my head back against his chest, I take in his handsome face and find my male grinning at me, a cheeky smile I match while those blue eyes crinkle at the corners. *I make him happy.*

"I'll hold you to that, Leonardo."

"Good little fae." My cheeks flush at that; I like his praise. Will never deny that. "Now tell me, Anaya. Why didn't Queen Amelia ever try to escape with you?"

My smile drops, and his brows furrow at the abrupt change. "Who said she didn't try?"

"So Ruben was being truthful? He said she ran with you, but I didn't believe..." At his trail off, I nod, and his head tilts to the side. "Can you tell me everything that happened? Whatever you remember is important."

Turning in his arms, I straddle his lap and place my forehead against his. Breathe in his every exhale while the man opens his mouth to speak, but a minute shake of the head stops him. "Let me answer your first half-dozen questions before you jump in and add another ten."

"I'll add that sass to my *later* list."

"Please do." Another deep breath and warmth spreads through me. His scent seems to have deepened even more. The cocoa and cloves—a rich spice and a bit earthy—settle over me like a thick blanket as I try to put together what memory I have of that age. Most of it is blurry at best. "I was young when this happened so I can't tell you exactly how—my recollection of the day is limited at best—but servants talk, and I've heard plenty of stories throughout the years. Of the first time she tried and the last."

"Not from your mother?" His expression is one of surprise.

"No. She would cut off any attempt on my part to leave *after* that day." Something I've always wondered about but never could pinpoint the why *until* Maman spoke of my mate. She knew about him. Who he was. But more importantly, my mother trusted the male meant for me. "*Your mate will be your peace. He will be everything you've ever dreamed of...sweet, caring, and will put you above all else. Including his hatred. His need for vengeance.*" Swallowing hard, I repeat each word just as she'd said them. Low, yet assured. "That was part of the last conversation we had, and her sole focus the entire time was reassuring me that you existed. That *you* were going to save me from King Larue and his vicious plans for me."

"Anaya." Just my name, but the raw, unadulterated love comes shining through so clearly. Vast and humbling, his true feelings make me gasp, even if this isn't the first time I've encountered them. I know he cares. That he loves me. Yet this is so much more than I could've hoped for: I'm his everything. "But when I met you—"

"I'd been lost. Focused on running away before they could marry me off." My truth. I'm a bit ashamed of how easily Larue manipulated me, but the one thing I'll never do to Leo is lie. Not now. Not ever. "For a while after our last conversation where Maman explained about the dark faes—the penance they carry for using and manipulating black magic—I was hopeful. Happy. Even while warning me, how she tried to teach me about the fae court's corruption, I couldn't move past the way Mom spoke about you. She already loved and accepted you for me."

"I hope one day you look back on this conversation with fondness and know how much I love you, my child. You're the only thing I've done right in this world."

"How did she know?"

Sitting back on his thighs, I shrug. "No clue, but I suspect she spoke to one of the few mages she still trusted or called in a favor."

"A favor? From whom?"

"From a powerful witch."

"Do you know who? Was it Silla?"

"No. That woman loathed my mother." Hiding my anger and disgust for Larue's sister is impossible. Every part of my being wishes to see her suffer, beg like my mother did whenever the horrid witch was displeased by her mere presence. "Silla hated her for no other reason than my maman was a royal, and her family was of a low ranking. Not that our queen cared; she accepted her mate and his family without hesitation. If anything, she loved Larue too much despite the horrid treatment."

"There's a reason for that, precious one." Without realizing it, my eyes—which I didn't realize were staring at the headboard behind him—snap to his. They're wary. A bit sad, and I know whatever he's about to unleash on me will hurt. "I'm sorry, Anaya."

Nodding, I exhale roughly, my heart beating erratically. "Tell me."

"Before I killed Ruben, he said a few things you need to know." Leo's hands on my back push me forward and keep me in place, his mouth slanting over mine. The kiss is soft. Just a few sweeps of his lips, an action that calms me, and the rigidness that had taken over me slips away. I melt for him. *This is what she meant. He's my center. My peace.* "Better?"

"Yes." And weirdly enough, I am. Maybe it's the knowing that I'll have answers to questions I've always asked myself. Maybe it's the knowledge that no matter what, Leonardo will stand by my side.

"Good little fae." I try not to as he pulls back a bit, but a tiny smile slips onto my face anyway. Moreover, I'm glad he ignores it and doesn't hold back from me either. I need to know what happened while I lay poisoned by Ruben on this very bed. "I'm humbled by your trust, and more than that, I know we'll get through this. Because the bad part will hurt, and the good will outweigh it all."

Grasping onto his words for dear life, I lift a hand to his chin and cup it. "I'm ready, Leo. What did Ruben say to you?"

"That Larue glamoured Queen Amelia, sweetheart. He wasn't her mate."

He's watching my reaction, taking in my every breath or shift in my body language, but I have nothing. "To be honest with you, I'm not shocked by this. If anything, it makes sense."

"Why do you say that?"

"Because I have no doubt, not a single one...you'd never hurt me. Physically or otherwise, and all that man did was humiliate her..." I take a pause, gauging myself and accepting the numbness that creeps in and takes over me. It's easier this way, to dissociate myself and take everything in as a bystander. Maybe not the healthiest way to deal with the truth, but for now, I'll lean on him and work my way through the rollercoaster I'm at the precipice of. "He humiliated her, Leonardo. Took great joy in her tears while those of a high ranking just ignored their queen's misery."

"Larue abused her in front of your people?"

"Not in the way you think. More of a *they didn't care* sort of way."

"What about your grandfather—"

"That man is dead to me." My tone's inflection is even, yet I couldn't bite back the volt of anger that rushed through me at the mention of the elder. Rapid. Harsh. Brutal ire. *He also abandoned us. Let Maman be hurt instead of protecting his only child.* The overwhelming emotion came and went quickly, a heated sear in my veins, but my king felt it and stiffened beneath me, his body on full alert. "Calm down, my king. I just hate the man."

"Why?" So gruff, his voice is a guttural growl while the arms wrapped around me tighten, pinning me against his rumbling chest. And while the sound of his reaction over my sudden distress should soothe me, this time I'm thrown by my father's voice in my head.

You have no voice or choice; remember that, my child.

Over and over again, I'm reminded. Hear the reprimand.

"He's dead. Larue and his son are dead."

You have no voice or choice; remember that, my child.

"Focus on me, Anaya. None of them will ever hurt you again."

You have no voice or choice; remember that, my child.

"Come back to me, baby. Tell me why you hate your grandfather?" Leonardo's question is simple enough; he's trying to refocus me, but the weight attached is a heavy one. It's just as crushing and difficult to express yourself when all the memories of your time at the fae court—with your family—bring forth the urge to scream. How do you articulate instead of cursing the very existence of the man who should've cared more about his daughter and less about staying in the good graces of the *king of idiots* who ruined said offspring?

The answer is that you don't. Can't.

And it isn't until that moment that I realize I'm mumbling something under my breath. It's on repeat, and I'm ashamed of it. Of my weakness.

You have no voice or choice; remember that, my child.

"Please let me in, precious one." Warm lips traverse from my eyelids to my cheeks and then down to my trembling mouth. From the right to the left, they don't stop until I let out a shaky breath and press a little more firmly. Just stay like that until I can focus enough through blurry eyes to meet his understanding ones, and that's when a deep and hurt-filled sob erupts. It leaves me and it rips me open, the years of pushing everything back and forgiving my maman for not leaving—even if I know she tried and failed in the past. "I've got you, Anaya. Your pain is mine. Your load is meant to be shared."

"Let me tell you what I remember of *that* day."

"I love you, my heart."

"As do I. You are my soul." Even though my hoarse reply pleases him, his heartbeat thumping harshly inside his chest, my male doesn't interrupt. He doesn't so much as move while I sit higher on his lap and bury my face in the crook of his neck, taking in his scent to calm my racing thoughts. I'm a paradox, from one extreme to the other as my entire being sags against him, but at the same time, I'm an eruption of repressed emotions.

Contradictory in every sense, and Leonardo senses this and tries his best to soothe me by running one hand up my back and cupping the back of my neck, holding me in place while his thumb rubs soothing circles on my skin. While the arm still around my waist pulls me impossibly closer, and it helps. I begin to get a hold of myself, my uneven breaths and my cries slowly becoming sniffles.

My shudders become languid until I just lie in his arms, absorbing his warmth. And while it takes a while, my male never hurries me. Just silently waits while the bond vibrates with understanding and so much love.

For me. For a fae princess hurt by her kingdom.

"Better?" he says, a deep whisper against my head.

"Yeah." His scent grows even thicker then; the chocolate and spice spreads throughout the room until it overwhelms in the best of ways. It drowns and gives anchor, and the longer I take in his comfort, the looser my lips become. I'm talking before I realize it, and it's cathartic. "...she failed, Leonardo. Maman ran away with me when I was a child, maybe no more than three at the time."

"Go on. I'm here."

"Being so young, I don't remember much, but I've never

forgotten the way she ran with me in her arms, nearly falling multiple times while begging me to keep quiet."

"It's time to play the silent game, young one," Maman whispers, her breathing labored. "The winner gets a special treat after dinner."

"Can I have a chocolat?"

"Chef Ninon may have given me one, but you have to beat me to earn it. Can you do that?"

"Oui!" I squeal. So excited.

"Quiet, ma cherie." Although her tone is chiding, Mom's smile is sweet. Always playful. "You don't want to lose so soon."

"And I remember winning that chocolat, being so excited once we reached the building with a large yellow door a little while later. Mom was so happy, her entire being radiated excitement until we stepped inside and found Father was waiting for us. And you know who was beside him? Who helped track her down?" It's rhetorical, but Leonardo whispers a low *no* anyway. "Beside him, once again abandoning his daughter, was my grandfather, both men very angry."

"How did he find you? Where were you?"

A small shrug. "No clue. Don't remember anything after that."

"What do you mean—"

Sitting up, I meet his stare while placing a finger over his lips. "I have no other memories from that day or most of my earlier years, to be honest, but when I woke up and Maman came in to help me get dressed, she wasn't the same anymore. Queen Amelia became quiet and subdued after that, almost nonexistent, while Larue grew in power, as did Ruben. He treated her as if she were lower than dirt. He didn't care about the woman who raised him, and now I know why. Sadly, it all makes sense."

"I'm sorry, precious one," Leonardo says while giving my finger over his lips a few soft kisses and nips, then he lowers it. Places our now entwined hands over his stomach and gives it an affectionate squeeze. And through it all, not once does he lose eye contact with me, letting me have clear access to his misplaced remorse. To an agony that matches my silent one. "I'm so sorry I didn't come for him sooner. I could've—"

"Not your fault, Leonardo. You're here now, and that's all that matters."

"I vow to make this right. I'll give back what's been taken from you."

Not that I don't appreciate the sentiment, because I do, but alarm bells are going off in my head and I swallow hard. My eyes narrow. "What do you mean by that, Leo? What haven't you told me?"

"I need you to understand that they cannot hurt either of you again. Ruben and Larue are dead, just like Silla will be soon enough."

She nods, then tilts her head to the side at my wording. Her expression is more curious than worried. "Tell me. Whatever it is, I'll be okay with you by my side."

"Amelia isn't dead, Anaya. Your mother is alive, and I vow it on my life that I will find her."

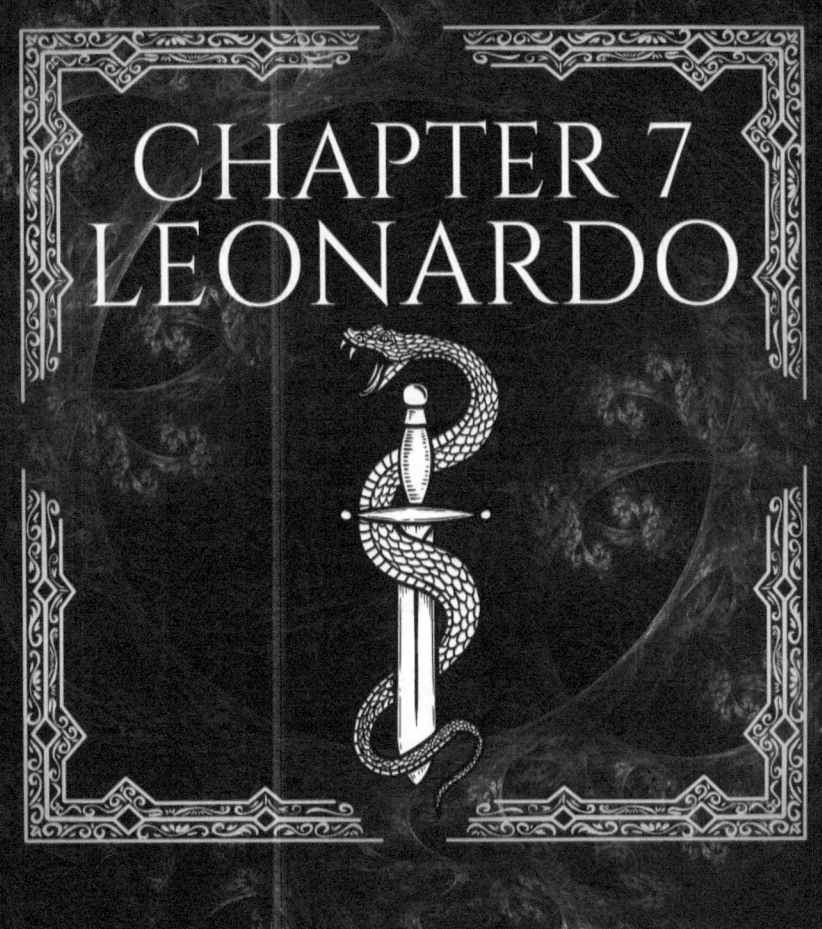

CHAPTER 7
LEONARDO

S he just looks at me.

No emotion. Not a single sound.

It's as if she's comatose, refusing to fall apart, yet her breathing's harsh and her posture rigid.

Anaya's on my lap but lost inside her head, and I hate that I'm the one who hurt her this way. But I refuse to lie to her, much less continue to keep my mate in the dark, when reuniting with her mother will bring her so much joy in the end. Right some of the wrongs committed against her.

They both deserve some happiness after what those animals put them through.

"Talk to me, precious one. How can I help you work through this?"

For a few minutes, she stays still while my hands rub up and down her arms, then down to her thighs before starting the process all over again. My mate's side of the bond is quiet, not a single vibration or emotion, but I understand that the shock is holding her captive.

From sadness to hope, to anger, and then elation at the possibility.

It's a painful kind of happiness I can relate to. I understand the years of pain and know how the hole left in your heart by a loved one's departure changes you, but having the chance to see them—to physically feel those you lost once again—is a blessing many are never given.

I went through this reaction the first time I dreamed of my parents after their deaths.

Young and still reeling from being left behind, I walked through my dream and connected to their resting place in the afterlife. They were waiting for me with huge smiles on their faces; I experienced the sense of a hug and the comfort of home, and I'm forever thankful that my Wiccan powers allowed me such a privilege, as short a visit as it was.

While the physical realm is binding, the spiritual plane allows us to play and bend while roaming freely. It gave me a bit of closure, and that respite from my pain allowed me to put one foot in front of the other while I trained to be king.

Just the same as when my father's presence looms close; the ceremony with my sisters being the perfect example before I met my queen. Because spirits can answer a call, they visit and bring with them the connection you've missed while taking a bit of the pain away, and Anaya now has the possibility of much *more.*

Her mother is alive, but lost. Can be a part of her life the right way.

"How, Leonardo? How is this possible?" my girl croaks, her voice heavy with hurt yet there's a small tinge of hope, too. "It just can't be. My mother lies within her garden, her ashes laid to rest among the white lilies, and I've mourned her there. All these years, I've cried for her eternal rest."

"That's what we need to find out, love." Finally, those violet eyes see me. Her ears twitch to let me know she's paying attention, too. "Ruben admitted that Larue glamoured your mother into believing that she was his mate and his maman with the help of a powerful witch. My guess is Silla helped him, then they killed the woman who birthed the spineless asshole."

"But why make us think she'd died? To what gain when they had it all."

"My guess is he wanted absolute control. With her out of the way, no one could clamor for the rightful monarch."

She's shaking her head, lips pursed. "It doesn't work that way, Leonardo. He was given a transfer of power. The faes recognized him as a carrier of the sacred blood."

"So he kept her nearby? Close enough to use?"

"He bled my maman the entire time." If devastation had a picture, her face would be it, and I hate myself for putting her through this. Tears fill her sad orbs, but they don't fall yet. She's fighting back her emotions to get through this conversation. *I'm going to take care of you, my precious fae. I'm so sorry.* "They used black magic against my people."

"I think it's worse than that, Anaya." I'm remembering Ruben's words between pitiful cries for a mercy I didn't grant. *If she dies, the real heir will step into her powers. The crown isn't handed over in the physical sense but manifests, and all faes would drop to their knees before Anaya. She would take what's mine.* "You would've risen without Larue tricking the court. The same powers he claimed to have been granted by Amelia before death would've manifested in you, and that's something they couldn't permit. You were the key to unmasking them, but by keeping your mother hidden and you thinking she'd died, he controlled the narrative. Controlled the rightful heir and planned to continue doing so by marrying you off to Brice, another loyal servant."

"He drank from her."

That stops me cold. "What do you—"

"He drank from her," she hissed from between clenched teeth as the first tears rolled down her flushed cheeks. "That is how he carried the sacred blood. It *was* a part of him, but because he stole her life's essence. Goddess!" Hands fisted in her locks, she pulls, and that's when my mate finally breaks.

Anaya's pain slams into me—volatile and open—as her petite body is wracked by sobs. As the years of hurt pour out of her in curses: for her dead father, for the man who played the part of an asshole brother, and then for what her mother's lived through. She blames the court's elders and their misogynistic views, and then she just cries for everything taken from her.

And through it all, I hold my beautiful mate and give her the one thing she's been without for a long time: comfort.

"I love you, sweet girl. We'll get through this and find her. I'll bring her home to you." My arms wrap around her, tucking her against my chest while I absorb every painful shudder. Feed her my unending admiration through our bond. *My strong little queen.* "I vow it, Anaya. You will be reunited with your mother."

I get a minute nod against my shirt as she shifts her face to my neck, burying her nose there. Her breathing is labored and rapid, a small wheezing sound filtering past her cherry lips, but that soon becomes hiccups the more she breathes me in.

My scent soothes her. Calms her enough that my treasure falls asleep gripping me just as tight as I hug her, Aya's body finally succumbing to exhaustion. And while I lay her down and then cover her body with a blanket, I make another promise to the quiet room.

"Your enemies are mine now, and I'll bring you their heads as an offering. The world will have a cleanse, and it'll be in your name." Leaning over, I place a final kiss on the corner of her mouth before pulling back. "So mote it be."

WHAT GREETS me on the training grounds is nothing short of amusing. *Theodore's been busy.*

There are hundreds of vampire guards standing in a semi-circle around their king while three men kneel on the harsh ground. The prisoners are not bound, just naked, and their bodies show signs of multiple fang marks—missing chunks—while bright red blood oozes from each quarter-sized wound.

They look painful.

Not big enough to kill them, but enough to deliver tremendous discomfort while they tremble at their king's feet. More so when I take a good look at the area, a rubble-filled section that's speckled with fragments of blood and what looks to be dried flesh. *Sacrificial.* Then, there's the tall wooden rods protruding from the ground. Thick and splintered, they're placed in the perfect position to watch the sun rise over the horizon.

Moreover, they don't see me as I approach, but Theo and Tero tilt their heads in my direction. They sense the shift in vibrations as I take my place behind the first man with my favorite opal dagger in hand.

Its hilt warms in my hand while the sky above becomes turbulent. As if nature is matching my wrath, and those guards who witnessed the killing of the imposter prince shift a step back.

Lighting strikes not far from where we stand, the grassy area burning to a crisp as a sharp cry fills the air—the sound of a scared man who senses danger but cannot see it.

All three men release a pathetic sound akin to a whimper and Theodore's face thunders, his expression one of disgust that is mirrored by Tero.

One of the three shifts a bit, tilting his head behind him as much as he can without drawing too much attention to himself. He finds nothing. Not a single stone is out of place, even as the tip of my blade hovers close to his neck.

Just a few inches.

Yet nothing. He can't find the threat.

Another thing I've mastered over the last century. Since the day my gift presented itself, the anger and pain fueling my magic, I learned to project the ability to become invisible past my body. I've made it possible to extend and encompass anything within my grip, allowing it to become one with me and unseen by the eye.

You will never know I'm there until I allow it.

"Let's begin." Theo's voice reverberates throughout the field, his ire palpable, and the vampires present hiss before baring their necks. It's a sign of respect, the ultimate trust between a king and his people. "Who paid you to betray your king? My family?"

"Your Majesty, I'm so—"

"Silence!" He's looking at me as he says this, and I bring the dirtied, blood-tipped blade across the idiot's throat. I saw through multiple layers of vampiric flesh, ignoring the gurgling sounds leaving his throat—from one side to the other—until his head hangs back at an awkward angle in my hold.

Held by a few vertebrae that I'll snap clean off when the time comes.

His ability to scream, much less verbally cry for mercy, is gone. There's no windpipe left, yet I can't kill him this way. It's painful, but the undead can only truly cease being through direct contact with sunlight, fire, or special blades with the ability to cut through hardened flesh.

Like the one in my hand, yet I won't end him so soon. Not until they tell me a story.

Because like all creations; vampires are still part human. Or were at some point, and that comes with weaknesses.

No creature is infallible. We all have limitations. And the opal dagger given to me as a special gift and bathed in red twice over will help him cross into the afterlife where Hades, Thanatos, and Aries await.

Their pain will bring me joy.

My sister made sure of that with her thoughtful present. After walking out of Anaya's room, her small body burritoed within a soft blanket, I met her at the foot of the stairs. Gabriella was waiting for me, a large smile on her face, but there was no amusement coming through our sibling connection.

If anything, her aura vibrated with barely contained rage while Gabby's red eyes shifted to a glass atop a small table the same style as the one inside the throne room, but this time the color differed and it represented purity in white. *"Have fun, brother."*

That's all she said before walking away, tapping the statement-piece furniture with a manicured finger and then disappearing around the corner, leaving me with a golden chalice and a thick, near-black substance inside of it.

"Answer me." One by one, his army drops to one knee, hands on their chests while the prisoners' whimpers grow. Well, two of them. The third tries to fight my hold, but I don't ease up. If anything, I jam the sharp end of the knife through what's left of his trachea and leave it there to bob with every unsuccessful swallow.

More blood pours out of him.

Draining him bit by bit of the substance he needs to live, his last meal a complete waste.

"H-how?" the one to my left asks, and I'm kind enough to yank the dagger out of his accomplice and embed it into his cheek with a quick, harsh flick of my wrist. It's also then that I manifest, my body appearing behind the three, and the fear in their eyes is heady.

"Does that answer your question, asshole?" I growl, every word dripping in my ire. "Now answer your king. Who the fuck sent you to help that dickless waste of space to hurt my mate?"

"She'll kill us." This comes from the man to the right; he's shaking the hardest. Pure, unadulterated fear seeps from his every pore and I inhale deeply, the beast in me rising to the surface.

Every man has one, no matter the species.

The ancient blood in my veins throbs, and I feel the hunger for vengeance grow with each choking breath the man still in my grip lets out. Like Xadiel and Theodore, I protect what's mine, and that's where Silla underestimated me. She doesn't understand the true bond between mates, her connection to Uncle Roberto being one-sided, and even then, I'm not so sure he wasn't glamoured like Amelia.

Because while they may be mates, there's no true bond. And if there ever was one, it's died a slow and painful death.

No true bonded pair would allow the other to be hurt, much less do the hurting.

"She's not the one you should be afraid of."

"Chiara and Silla are—"

"How are they connected?" Theodore asks. He steps up to the still-unharmed vampire and kneels so they're eye to eye. "Tell me, Giulio. You have my word your beloved will be spared and no harm will come to your bloodline."

"My Lord..." The man named Giulio breaks off into sobs then, shame and repent in his every word. "I'm so sorry. They begged me to help, and when I denied them, they threatened my beloved and—"

"Is she safe now?"

"Yes, my king."

"Then tell me—what connection do Chiara and Silla have?"

Beside him, the two I've injured protest, making what complaints they can, but I help the noise level drop when I take what's left of the one in the middle's head, and with a solid twist, rip his head off. His eyes are open wide and set on me, but that changes when I toss the cranium toward a pyre started by my sister.

When Gabriella arrived, I have no clue nor do I care, but I appreciated the thoughtfulness. Find her antics amusing as she flicks the lighter in her hand on and off without a care in the world. Not worried the least bit about being hurt herself.

The head rolls and then sizzles, burning to ash within seconds of meeting the fire. His body follows the same demise, a useless creature killed for its stupidity and greed. Because I have no doubt they'd been promised money and a higher rank within their world, but what they didn't account for was me.

For how much I love the beautiful little fae who fell asleep in my arms with tears rolling down her soft cheeks.

"Answer him, Giulio. Don't force my hand."

The scared man swallows harshly, eyes brimmed with red tears that will never fall. "She's Silla's daughter. Hers with General Veltross."

CHAPTER 8
LEONARDO

"She's Silla's daughter. Hers with General Veltross."

W hat. The. Fuck.

That's...

My eyes meet my sister's, then flick to her mate, and they are each wearing the same murderous expression. It vibrates through them, a volatile and unhinged hatred only that name—the piece-of-shit family—can bring forth.

"Will you ever have children, Aunt Silla? I want a little cousin,"

I say after entering the kitchen, finding her at the sink, and looking out the window. She's pensive, has been for a few days now, and jumps when I tap her shoulder. "Did you hear me?"

"I'm sorry, piccolo. What did you ask?" She lifts a hand and pushes my red locks back from my face before cupping my chin. "How was your training today, my young king."

"Good, but I'm exhausted."

"Thirteen summers and growing, you'll get there, kid. How about a snack?"

"Please." Leaning closer, she kisses my cheek and then turns to serve me one of her bombolone with a cup of hot chocolate, adding a little cinnamon to the top. Just how I like it. "But what about kids? I'd love a little cousin."

"You want a cugino?" Her tone is off. Almost shocked.

"Yes. They'd be another sibling."

A touch of sadness flashes across her face, but it's gone before I can ask. Her smile is back as she places my snack on the counter next to me, bumping her shoulder with mine. Elbowing me playfully, too. "Let me talk to Uncle Roberto about it. Who knows, I might just surprise you one day."

Fuck her. She did. More than, actually.

I'm angry. Fuming.

Every member of that family has been a problem, and it seems Brice and Ruben were right to warn me that a snake in the grass has many friends. Those who are willing to help and corrupt nations over the preconceived notion that the world owes them when nothing could be further from the truth.

Their mistake. From the fallen general of the vampire army to his daughter Elise, and now the last descendant in Chiara: a tribrid.

Part witch, fae, and vampire.

An abomination, and not because of the mixing of species—our entire family is now blended and thriving and blessed—but because of her black heart.

"Don't say another—" the asshole with my blade sticking out of his cheek tries to interject, but Tero strikes, wrapping himself around the enemy guard and squeezing. He's shifted fully, his albino animal unhinging its jaw and swallowing the top of his head. Tero pauses when he reaches the hilt of my knife and gives a low hiss from the back of his opened jaws.

I step closer and pat the vampire's uninjured cheek while removing the weapon from his flesh. My slap is a little condescending, a little unhappy about not ending him myself, but I nod at the serpentine shifter to continue after stepping back.

The vampiric king's right-hand proceeds to fully encompass the head before using its serrated teeth to embed and then cut his head off. A little at a time. Painfully so. He doesn't pause or adjust the man, simply removing the head before slithering over to the pyre and dropping the offering. Does the same with the body, but not in one go as I did.

First are the arms and then legs and lastly, his torso. The constrictor kept his eyes on me throughout, much to his lord's amusement, as if to show me how it's done.

My response—I snort at him and shake my head. "It's not polite to show off, Tero."

He tilts his head to the side and hisses at me before shifting his gaze to the lone survivor. Scales vibrate the longer he watches him, revealing the man underneath until his top half is human while the bottom coils, ready to attack. "Tell us everything, Giulio. How long have you known the traitorous bitch was that scum's daughter?"

How the fuck did we miss this? All this time she's been hiding with the Rossi coven. Did Christopher know?

How did she end up with them, to begin with?

Those questions roam my head in a constant loop. So much unanswered, my poor mate in danger—our entire family and kingdoms at risk—but then Giulio clears his throat.

"They came to me a few days ago." His face is pallid, even for a vampire, as he looks into the fire. Accepting his future. "Jenco and Edo cornered me during a patrol shift change; I was coming and they were going. Said they needed a favor from me."

"What kind?" I ask, and he shifts his eyes to me for a second, then looks away. More shame. Heavier fear. "Who did they want you to let through?"

"One named Chiara and then an older one. Don't remember much about the latter; she kept quiet."

"Was her name Lena?"

"Yes. That's what I believe she called her, King Moore."

"And you let them onto my lands?" Theodore thunders, chest heaving and eyes blood red, but he settles a bit when Gabriella takes her place beside him, her hand is on his arm, holding his beast back. "What the fuck were you thinking?"

"I didn't."

"What do you mean, Giulio? This isn't making any sense." Gabriella's tone is gentle while she continuously runs her fingers up and down the vampire king's arm. Too deceptively calm, and the man reacts to it. Sways toward her. "Explain yourself."

"When they arrived, I was under the impression it was a *sexual* kind of visit. What's commonly known as a booty call now, and not the arrogant young woman who arrived demanding to know where every royal member's chambers were. Where Princess Anaya slept."

"Keep going, Guard. Tell your queen everything."

"Stop," I interject, staring at my sister and brother-in-law. Neither complain about the interruption. "Every vampire not kneeling needs to leave."

The meaning behind that hits without my needing to explain, and their king whistles once before Tero empties the field. No one but the four of us and the guard kneeling are needed now, just to be safe. I'd do the same with my army, especially after proof of there being a few traitors.

Only then do I wave him on. "Continue."

"I swear, I didn't let that Chiara pass. Didn't trust her, or the men I considered friends at one point, by then." He takes in a deep breath and lets it out slowly, body shuddering. "Chiara threatened me, ordering Edo and Jenco to bring my wife when I refused them, and they did, forcing my heart to kneel at *her* feet. Bianca is an innocent, my queen. She was so scared as the woman held her near the southern borders, close to the tree line where the early-morning sunbeams are the strongest."

"Then what happened?" He's not picking up on the darkness in my sister's tone but continues to respond to the call he's under. "Help me, help you."

At that, his head meets the ground as he prostrates himself at his monarch's feet. Giulio is blubbering; you can barely understand him, but a few things come through clearly:

"I stood my ground, but they cut my beloved's cheek. I begged them to leave. Warned them they wouldn't get away with this." Tero's almost-white brows furrow, his face pinched tight at Giulio's words as if remembering the day in question himself. "They grabbed me and forced me down beside my heart, but then footsteps drew closer and King Theodore's voice carried toward our location. He was with Tero. I tried to scream, but Edo covered my mouth while Jenco choked my mate. Amid the attack, I lost sight of Chiara, and I have no idea where she went after that."

"That's all?"

"Yes, Your Majesties. And I accept whatever punishment you deem justified; all I beg is that you don't hurt my Bianca."

For a few minutes, no one speaks but looks are shared. This man isn't a traitor, but someone forced into a horrible situation, and while he failed to tell his king what happened immediately, that doesn't negate Giulio standing his ground. He didn't betray them by allowing the traitorous cunt entry.

Which means there are more dirty vampires.

"Get up, and breathe easy. I will not kill you today." With shaky legs, Giulio stands while his king appraises him. He's a lot calmer now, and so am I. "You will be demoted and under constant watch for a very long time, but you will appease me. You will get me every name involved, how they betrayed me, and report to Tero. He has a list of his own you will corroborate on; is that understood?"

"Yes, my king. Thank you, Your Majesties."

"Then get to work. This pyre needs to be fed."

CHAPTER 9

Anaya

"You're the only thing I've done right in this world."

Consciousness seeps in slowly, my memory of Maman becoming faint as my languid body picks up certain shifts in the air—while my lungs expand, taking in the scent of chocolate, spice, and lastly *ash*, the latter of which causes my ears to twitch and one eye to crack open, searching the room for the person responsible for this peculiar combination.

It hurts at first. The lighting is too bright and my eyes burn, causing me to whine and burrow deeper into my haven because these blankets are the plushiest and softest things I've ever owned.

A gift from Isabella in her latest shipment of clothing, buried at the bottom of the largest box, and I found it this morning before getting dressed to meet with Leo's siblings. He laughed at the squeal I emitted and then gave a low snarl, grumbling over the gift not coming from him.

"Those noises are mine, precious one. Only my gifts can evoke those sexy fuck-me sounds."

I'd smiled at that then, and now my lips twitch just the same.

"I know you're awake, little fae." His deep, rumbling voice comes from the end of the bed and I try to look over, testing the brightness for a second time. Now it's a little better. Only stings a tiny bit, and I find my male sitting atop a high-back, ornate chair a few inches from the bedframe. His bare feet are up and his chest is on display, a few lingering drops of water from a shower clinging to his skin.

Why does he still smell like smoke after his shower?

His red hair seems mocha brown in its wet form, but a ray of light catches it at just the right angle, bringing forth a beautiful array of copper and deep auburn with touches of blond throughout. Then, that same lighting highlights his sharp jaw and the short beard my male's been sporting since I woke up.

He truly is a fine specimen.

Tall and muscular and currently giving me a playful grin as I watch him through slightly narrowed eyes. "Ready to sit up, or should I crawl in and warm up?"

Leonardo's giving me the opportunity here to demand space after our talk. I haven't forgotten; I'm aware we have so much more to discuss—to plan for—but I also need *him*. The pain in my heart hasn't ebbed, yet the kernel of hope and happiness at the knowledge I'll be reunited with my maman is helping me rationalize the past.

None of this *was* or *is* my fault. Not hers either.

This is an opportunity many don't get after losing a loved one. I'm aware and will appreciate it, work until I bleed to find her, and walking beside me through each step will be this wonderful man. The sole person who can settle my thoughts. Who gives me strength and feeds my need for love, and right now, every rampant emotion—my connection to him—cries out for his touch.

To lean on him. To not get caught up in the hurricane of emotions without a way to ground myself, because I didn't ask for help. For a respite.

Because I didn't voice just how deeply and completely I hunger for him.

"Come to me, my mate. I want to cuddle."

"As you wish, my queen." Standing, he pushes the chair back and lets a white towel drop before lifting the end of my soft blanket, exposing me to the cooler air. I shiver, rubbing my right foot over the back of my calf, but then he's over me and I'm pinned—safe within my favorite place in the world.

Under him. Surrounded by him.

"Hi," I say in a low whisper. "How long was I asleep?"

"Two days."

"What the—"

"Relax, love. You needed the rest." Lowering his face to mine, I'm given a proper morning kiss. Slow and sweet, his mouth moves over mine a few times before his warm tongue flicks my bottom lip, a silent demand for entry I grant without pause. It's tender how he explores and caresses while I savor his taste, our tongues intertwining without any sense of rush or worry about what's happened.

I need this. Didn't know how much until Leo's naked body slips between my parted thighs, his thick cock lying atop my slick heat. He deepens the kiss then, his mouth dominating and taking while one large hand grips my left thigh and wraps it around his lower back.

Those same fingers knead and squeeze as they wander from my calf to my hip and then slip between us to press two thick fingers over my clit. Just pressing. Feeling me throb beneath the pads of his digits; I'm sensitive there. The way he claimed me after I marked him, and every time after, is ever present in the slight soreness each time I shift, but that only heightens my arousal.

I drip for him. Clench in need, and he must feel the quick flex of my entrance because he notches the bulbous tip and gives a short thrust. Leonardo feeds me a few inches, a taste to tease and drive me crazy with frustration, but not enough to come. He does this once, twice...five times, and then backs out as he continues to spread my wetness at a languid pace.

"I promised you two days ago that I'd claim you again. That once you left this bed, you'd never doubt my devotion to you ever again."

"Never did." A moan. Slight whimper.

"Then let me reaffirm that conviction." No hurry as his cock, slick in my juices, slides through my labia and bumps my clit. He's gripping the base with the same fingers he'd pressed against me, and each time he does, it's like a pleasurable shock to my system. I can't contain each moan that slips through my parted lips, or how I'm panting, my nails digging into his bicep in a silent plea, one he shakes his head at.

"Use your words, my precious one. I want to hear your need for me."

"Claim me." Two words, but nothing else is needed.

Heated stare on mine, Leonardo watches me through hooded eyes as he slides inside me again, this time to the hilt, gifting me with that familiar burn that set off pinpricks of pleasure throughout my body. I feel full, so content, and moan in appreciation. "My perfect girl. Feel so good."

"Will it always be like this?"

"In this life and every single one that follows."

His body lies over mine, covering me from head to toe while his girth flexes as he pulls out, dragging against my walls before punching back in. This is how he loves me, slow and deep while his lips kiss everywhere he can reach. Eyelids, cheeks, my mouth—my neck, where he bites down hard enough to break the skin, and I shatter, the orgasm slamming into me with the same intensity as his love.

But that isn't enough for him, and my male continues, not picking up the pace but pumping in deep while one hand slips between us and presses down on my abdomen, feeling the imprint of his cock as my stomach bulges. It turns him on, how much smaller I am to him, and I can't deny being grabbed, used, and manipulated to his liking turns me on too.

How he completely overwhelms me with his size.

Gives me no choice but to take the pleasure he so freely gives, and as I tighten around him again, his mouth skims my ear. His heavy breathing—those sexy male grunts—steal my breath.

"There has never been, nor will I ever desire, another female, Anaya. You are where I begin and end. You are the very air I breathe, my precious one, and I'd rather die than give my seed to another." His pace picks up, slamming in and out of my sensitive core now as he chases his pleasure, pulling aftershocks from me. I'm trembling, lips parted on a silent scream as my hands clutch him closer, fingernails breaking the skin of his back as he thrusts in deep a final time and stills. "My mate. My queen. Let me live for you."

Each word is a guttural plea.

His groan is so deep it travels through me.

But more beautiful than those reassuring truths is the feel of his spend filling me to the brim.

No one else will ever experience moments like this with either of us. We are one.

It takes us a few hours to make it downstairs and into the dining room where we find Leo's sisters sitting beside one another and whispering. The words between them are fast, no more than gibberish from where I stand, but my eyes are drawn in by their respective glasses. One holds a long-stemmed champagne flute, the contents of which look like blood—red and thick from exposure to oxygen—and the other drinks sparkling water while holding back a grimace between sips. So different, yet the same, and it's amusing to see how each mimics the other's mannerisms.

Twins in looks, but it's the identical behaviors that stop me.

I've never spent time with them together, always apart, and this is different.

They talk with their hands. They roll their eyes the same way mid-response before tossing their red hair back. How both pairs of eyes: one blue, one green, snap in our direction simultaneously and narrow the moment Leo clears his throat. "Who are we burning at the stake today?"

"You, if your mate allows it," Gabriella answers, not missing a beat, giving me a wink. "Or did you have other plans today?"

"I do."

"I already know, and we'll be leaving with you after my nap. Xadiel won't allow us to depart otherwise." Isabella smiles sweetly at her sibling, amused by the low growl beside me. "Behave, brother. You wouldn't want your mate to think you're a brute."

"She likes my uncouth behavior just fine."

"She can speak for herself, too," I interject, and that sets the two women off, high-fiving each other before Isa pushes the chair beside her out. Points at it and then me, while Gabriella picks up her phone and sends a text. "Thank you."

"And where am I allowed to sit?" Leo barks, eyes shifting around to notice two missing members of the family. No wolf. No vampire.

Not so much as a guard standing watch on this floor. At least, I don't see any.

Ignoring her brother, Isa tilts her head in my direction, her lip twitching at the corner. "Nice to see you again, Aya. How was your morning shower?"

"Refreshing."

"I'm sure. You missed quite the interesting breakfast."

"Did I?" Something I've learned since meeting Isabella and Gabriella: they're both playful with those they care about. Never in a mean way. The jokes, innuendos, and moments like these once again show me that I'm part of something. That I have a real family, and if in the past I wondered what a true sibling relationship would feel like —if Ruben didn't hate me—it'd be like this. "Although I get the feeling I missed a bonfire, instead. The scent of ash permeated my room, even after Leo's shower before I woke up."

"How can you signal out the scent—"

"I'm sensitive. It's that way for most fae, but being a royal, mine picks up on differences others might not. Like in Chiara's case." My nose crinkles at the memory. "Even while living on fae lands where I dealt with the pungent smell daily, it was hard to keep a straight face among Larue's closest circle. Raw sewage isn't something one can get accustomed to.

"How did we miss that?"

I shrug, not understanding either. "My guess is dark magic."

"Pure-hearted faes are easier to distinguish when you know what you're looking for, my little Aya. Those with the dark sickness reek of it—it clings to their being—and you need to heed that warning, young one. Those high-priced sentences are paid for by their magical essence, rotting them from within, for wielding forbidden magic."

"How long have they been practicing blood manipulation, Anaya?" Isabella asks, and beside her, Gabriella gives a low snarl. "Did you ever see them bleed anyone?"

"This started long before I was born. When our lands were allies, not enemies."

"Gods. We should've eliminated—"

"Gabriella, there are good faes there. Not all are evil." Their mates walk in at the tail end of that statement. Their expressions are grim. "Identifying the pure-hearted ones becomes easier when you know what you're looking for. The stench, the dark seal, is unmistakable—permeates everything they touch—and no amount of expensive perfume or spell can cover it for long. That's why I picked it up on Chiara and Lena; it just took me a minute to decipher why my being was repulsed by them. At the time, so much was going on around me and I—"

"Breathe, Anaya." Gripping the back of my neck, Leo turns my face in his direction. When he took a seat beside me, I don't know, but I'm thankful, nonetheless. "I'm so proud of you. No one here picked up on such an important fact. It's because of you that we know Chiara's the daughter of Silla and a vampire enemy to the crown. That entire bloodline is a curse."

"Did you say Veltross?" *Why does that name seem familiar?*

"Do you know them, Anaya?" Theodore cuts in before anyone else can ask. "Meet anyone in the family?"

"I want to say *yes*, but at the moment I don't remember when. But that's a name I've heard multiple times over the..." I trail off, recalling something. It's not the clearest memory, but my gut tells me it's important. "A woman. That's where the name comes from."

"Are you sure?" They exchange glances between themselves, but it's Xadiel who speaks this time, the same gruff, yet warm timbre I heard the day they stormed into Larue's building. When he saved me from Brice and the head scientist.

"I am."

I've been tasked with delivering refreshments to Brice's office at my father's request with the help of one of the court's live-in maids. She carries the wine and glasses, while a specifically designed charcuterie board weighs my arms down. Between the butcher block, fine China with a few spreads, and the slippery crackers between cold cuts: I want to toss the entire thing against the nearest wall.

"I'll knock, ma princesse. Let me—" We're stopped by a loud female moan. The high-pitched squeal reverberates down the hall, and we look at each other. Both uncomfortable. "Maybe we should come back?"

I'm shaking my head before she finishes. "No. We're dropping this off."

"It's for the best." Her expression shows how much she disagrees with her own statement, and I understand this is awkward, but my father will punish her to hurt me if we don't follow his instructions.

"We'll make it quick." Striding forward, I take the lead and knock on the door. All noises cease, and the heavy sound of footsteps

nears until the door is yanked open, revealing a bare-chested Brice with a small female behind him.

"She was a brunette with a small linear scar near her—"

"Temple," Isabella finished for me. "Who do we know with a scar like that? That fits the description?"

"That fuckin…!" Gabriella snarls at the same time her mate moves toward her, his speed faster than I could follow with my eyes, and he's cupping her face. His grin is dark and sinister. "That family—"

"It's time we hunt, pretty girl. Let's go play." She nods, and he lifts her at the same time Xadiel pulls Isa's chair back, each couple exiting the room while calling out that they'll meet us at a later time. One says soon, while the other promises later tonight.

Moreover, we're alone within seconds, and I'm lost. Have no clue what just happened.

"Leo?"

"We're going home, sweetheart. We're going to put an end to this."

CHAPTER 10
LEONARDO

"Welcome home, Your Highnesses," Augusto greets us when we step through the portal, his smile as wide as his mate's and Isotta's, who stands beside the two nearly vibrating with excitement. She's happy to see me, but her reaction is all for the tiny fae in my arms who taps my shoulder, silently asking me to put her down.

I don't, though. Instead, I kiss her cheek and pretend to not understand the gesture.

"Thank you, my friend."

"Thank you. Happy to be home," we answer in unison, the trio watching us as my mate pats me a little harder this time. Less incon-spicuous. *Tap. Tap. Tap.* "Um, Leo…"

"Yes, precious one?" More like hitting now, her knuckles digging in a bit, and it takes everything in me not to laugh at her mild annoyance.

Am I doing this on purpose? Yes.

Am I ashamed of playing such childish games? Not one bit.

Especially when I get to hold on to her a little longer.

"Can you put me down please?"

"Why?"

"Because I'm going to bite you if you don't, my king. And trust me, you won't like it this time." At my raised brow, her fangs drop, and the imp strikes before I can kiss her, biting the tip of my ear. The very edge, and I can't deny it stings. She pierces the cartilage and shakes her head a bit, tearing the skin and I hold strong, not giving in to her choice of violence.

You're going to pay for that, Anaya. Another mark against you.

In my head, I hear a giggle. The bond thrums with amusement.

Put me down so I can greet Isotta and Annett, my love. I missed these two females.

That warms my heart. How much she cares for them, the same way they adore her.

It was crystal clear the day my female left these lands while I hunted my escaped prisoners, their anger at her departure filling me with pride. They accepted my queen wholeheartedly.

Something crystal clear the moment I set her down and they rush to say hello, each woman placing their foreheads against my mate, whispering how much they've missed her.

We've been home on Wiccan territory for a week now, and there's been no word from Theodore or Gabriella. Not from Isabella or Xadiel, either.

I'm not worried about them, though. Tero has done his job and visited twice, each time giving me a verbal report on his findings and assuring me they are safe.

"Silla was spotted in London two days ago, close to werewolf territory." We're sitting inside my office, the constrictor's scales becoming visible with each intermediate vibration. His entire body is wound tight, his leg shaking as he hands me a folded note. Roberto eyes it, face pinched tight. "But before a wolfen guard who'd taken the weekend off to spend with his mate could approach, she took off, blending with the crowd and then vanishing altogether."

"She's smart. I'm also positive news of Ruben's death has reached her by now." My uncle makes a croaky sound then, pulling my attention toward him. His finger's pointing at a legal pad on my desk and the pen beside it; I hand the items over and watch him scribble a quick note.

Silla wanted you to see her. I have no doubt that was done on purpose.

"But why? What's her angle?" Tero asks after reading Roberto's writing. "Seems idiotic to expose yourself like that, especially with hunters searching for her daughter and the fae male Chiara helped escape."

I haven't spoken to my uncle about his *mate's* offspring, and I take in the shock on his face.

The utter betrayal and devastation.

"You didn't know about her?" His head shakes at my question, his hand flying across the page and his writing is sloppy—angry.

What daughter? What are you talking about?

"Silla gave birth to a Veltross offspring over a century ago, zio.

89

How did that happen?" The more I think about it, the angrier I become. Did he help her hide it? "How the hell could you not know this?"

I didn't.

Goddess, I trusted and loved her, and she…

"Roberto, what do you remember of the time close to your brother's death?" Tero snaps his head to the side; he's listening to something beyond the door. "Did you spend any time apart?"

Footsteps draw near, then retreat, and then come back all within the span of a minute. The albino shifter holds back a laugh, and that's a reaction I've seen him have multiple times around Anaya. He finds her quirks adorable, as does his wife, Isotta, Augusto's wife, and a few others who work for me.

The kitchen staff is happy to indulge her desire to learn how to cook.

The women's trainer is teaching her how to throw a proper punch in between jokes and laughs.

My uncle taps at the paper in front of me.

Two years before your father's murder, Silla and I separated for a year. She accused me of cheating on her after a woman I'd never seen in my life claimed to be my lover.
I didn't step out on her, Nephew. Never could disrespect our bond, but I always wondered about her sudden change of mind after no contact for so long. One day she was just back. As if nothing happened.

Before I can ask him any more questions, though, Anaya enters.

"It's time to take a small break, Leonardo. You've been in here for four hours." In her hands, there's a tray of sandwiches, some chips, and a few sodas. Isotta's behind her with cups of ice and empty plates. "You missed lunch."

"Thank you, little queen."

"You're most welcome, my king." While Isotta hands the men drinks and then food, my female prepares mine. It's a beautiful feeling to be taken care of this way, to have your mate serve your meal, but nothing is sweeter than the small Post-It note tacked on to the lip of my plate.

We have a date tonight, Leonardo.
I'm ready to pay for my list of sins.

Bites and kisses,
Anaya

"Did you eat, sweetheart?" I take a bite of the submarine sandwich, pretending to groan at the flavor profile of fresh mozzarella, deli meats, and balsamic vinaigrette—not her naughty promise. *My good girl is so responsible. I love your initiative, Aya.*

"I did..." she starts but then trails off; I find her staring at the still-folded note Silla dropped. "W-where did you get that?"

"Get what, precious one?" Violet eyes snap to mine, and I don't like what I see. Her trepidation. Fear. "What is it?"

"That's the royal fae army's stationary, Leonardo. I'd know that paper anywhere." *Who sent it? What does it say?*

I haven't read it yet.

She exhales roughly. *Give it to me, please.*

I do as she asks, handing it over while Tero and Roberto watch. We follow her every move, taking in the way she unfolds the note and then just as quickly spreads it face down atop my desk.

It's a blank sheet on both sides, not so much as a single smudge on it, but that changes when my mate uses the condensation from my glass to wet the paper. Slowly, it uncovers a hidden message.

One word. Four letters.

Mors.

Death.

"Maledicte!" I thunder, and a snap of thunder cracks the ground outside, a rapid storm building within my territory. The shelves across from me begin to thrum with the sudden whip of power, a new kind of sensation flowing through the room a second before a weathered tome breaks free and nearly smacks me in the face.

I catch it at the last moment. The harsh slap against my open palm warms the skin right before it lands on my desk with a muted, yet heavy thud. Pages flip and flutter from back to front before splitting down the middle, revealing an intricate map with a set of coordinates written in a messy script on one side, and a picture of a three-story building on the other.

I don't recognize them, much less know the area, but the gasp from the woman beside me puts me on high alert.

Anaya's holding a hand over her mouth and tears fill her eyes, her finger tracing down a yellow door. "How?"

We reached the building with a large yellow door...

"Is this the—"

"Yes. I could never forget the color or façade, how tall and imposing the entrance seemed." My mate's eyes widen and then close, her small hand reaching out to mine in her rush of anxiety—the unpleasant memories this brings to the surface. Intertwining our fingers, I squeeze them while she's lost inside her head, and Tero shifts in his seat, his animal side picking up on the dangerous energy now filling the room.

On her distress.

My uncle, though, simply watches with concern until he focuses on the map, and within seconds, it's clear that he, too, recognizes the place. Pain etches onto his face. Roberto's hands clench in his lap, and the man's reaction reminds me of his first days back on these lands.

Wounded. Cornered. Bitter.

What the fuck is going on?

"Talk to me, mate. Where's your head at?"

Without opening her eyes, her lips move. "That building is where they caught us when Maman escaped with me. Larue and Grandfather were there, imposing and throwing insults, and the latter threatened to drown her if Amelia didn't stop her *nonsense*. Her father told her he'd do the same to me in the lake behind the property if she didn't fall into line." Roberto stands and his chair topples, angry grunts coming from his tongueless mouth, but I don't look away from the woman who owns my heart. Her pain guts me. The bond is screeching with her distress. "They made her comply because of me, Leo. Everything was because of me."

A palm meets the wooden edge of my desk; it pins a piece of paper next to the map. My mate jumps at that, a snarl sitting on the tip of my tongue for causing her further distress, but Zio's writing stops me cold. Has the same effect on Anaya a few seconds later as she reads his message.

Gives her a small token of calm. A *hope* that wasn't there before.

Leonora knew her mother, Leo. At one point were friends.

Your parents had to have planted this before their deaths.

CHAPTER 11

Anaya

"**W**e're going to be okay, Aya. We've made it," Maman croons softly, her light footfalls traveling up a pathway lit by a break in the trees. The entrance is covered by large, imposing oaks that create a thick canopy where little light filters through. Yet for her, they sway and allow rays of sunshine to dot each stone paver as we walk up to a too-tall yellow door.

It's intimidating; the structure is tall, solid wood with a brass knocker at the center in a lion's head motif. The animal's mouth is open, its sharp incisors holding the brass handle.

"Are you ready for our new adventure, ma princesse? We're going to be so happy!"

Mom uses it and knocks three times; an audible click follows as the door opens slowly. It creaks, the old hinges loud, but then it doesn't matter as the moment we step inside, the smile vanishes from her face.

"Ma cherie, I've missed you," a voice I know says, and I tighten my grip on Maman's shirt. "Please close the door and follow me. We have much to discuss."

"Leave, Larue. I've given you everything—you've drank my very blood—there's nothing more to give."

"That's where you're wrong." Two men appear behind us and I'm ripped from my mother's arms, that horrid yellow door slamming closed, blocking off our escape. "I demand your soul, Amelia, and you've failed to deliver!"

"Release my daughter this instant!"

There's a soundtrack of crying. Someone is thrashing, but as I look at the two men holding my arms as I'm suspended above the floor by their grip, it's not me. But the high pitch is that of a child. Recognize the wail of pain as my own.

How can that be? Am I dreaming?

"Enough, Daughter. You will come home and stand beside your husband; this game is embarrassing." The deep timbre comes from my left; his nails dig into my tiny bicep and break skin. I feel the sharp sting. How he doesn't stop until I scream.

Yet my lips haven't moved.

I'm too aware to be the culprit of such a heartbreaking cry.

"You're helping him? You're turning your back on your daughter?" Maman's voice breaks, her hands shaking, and I catch the glint of a blade in her grip, something they haven't. "How could you?"

"And I'll do worse if you don't submit."

Eerie calmness fills the foyer, interrupted only by the scurrying of footsteps as they draw near. The person stops just out of sight, but their perfume is cloying. Too heavily floral.

"I'm not going back. Leave."

"Then you leave me no choice." Larue snaps his fingers, and

more royal guards infiltrate the space. *They come from all angles and grab Queen Amelia, dragging her outside while Grandfather picks me up and does the same.*

There's thrashing. Some pleading.

It falls on deaf ears as we pass through a long corridor and approach already-open French doors that lead outside to a lake. It's vast and looks deep, its water murky and cold.

"You have two choices, my love." Larue's sneer is evil, his expression gleeful. *"Come home and be my pet, my blood whore, or I drown the little future queen. Either way, I'll get what I want, but the dynasty ends here."*

"She's your daughter!"

"She's a fucking problem, Amelia." It's a hiss, the true feelings of a man who should love and protect his mate. His offspring. *"That child is a walking, breathing threat to—"*

"Touch her..." Maman says, her voice is lethal *"...and I'll show you what a true savage is. You know it's not an empty threat, either."*

Father's eyes narrow as a deep gouge appears on his cheek, the skin torn open jaggedly and oozing blood. A knife wound. *"You'll pay for that attack; I will never forgive you."*

"Don't force my hand, then," she grits out.

"Or maybe I'll break your spirit instead." A tray appears in the hand of a woman; I can't see her face, but something about her is familiar. Her dark hair and stature are ones I've seen. *"One cup is a poison, while the other will put her to sleep. Both will harm her, Amelia, make no mistake about it. I could toss her helpless body in the water and watch it sink; the added weight I'd tie around her neck will make sure of it."*

"Don't you dare!"

"Then come home, Daughter, or we end this in the most painful way for you." My pitiful body is released. I hit the ground, and another wail rips through the group as my hair is pulled and my head forced back. *"You chose, Amelia. Love, or utter heartbreak?"*

"It will always be love."

"Then kneel and kiss the ring. Show me how sorry you are."
She's forced to her knees by the kick of a loyal guard, her eyes flashing to me with sheer, pain-filled panic as her fangs drop and she bites her lips hard enough to break the skin. Immediately they shimmer with her blood, a few drops falling to the ground where a small bloom appears.

In slow motion, Maman leans forward and presses her lips against the large stone at the center of the ring. It shimmers as she does—every amulet in the room glows a lovely blue—as the ring's gem binds itself with her essence before a cold liquid drips into my mouth...

Wake up, Anaya. You've seen enough, child.

"Precious one," Leonardo calls out, his timbre soft as to not scare me, but I'm slammed back into the present so hard I gasp. Clutching my throat and coughing, I'm spluttering when my male wraps me in his arms and walks us over to a cuddler. There's one in every room, his decree, and he sits with me in his lap.

The dream—I've never felt anything like it before.

So real. So vivid.

"What happened?" He's stroking my blonde hair back, fingers skimming the tip of my left ear each time before moving onto the right side. "You saw something."

Not a question, but a statement. As if he understands what I don't.

"I was there." My voice is so low that even my ears twitch to catch the whisper. "Like a spectator in my own memory; I watched how they ambushed us and threatened my life. All this time I thought they wanted to drown her, but it was me Larue wanted dead. Saw me as a threat."

"You are the rightful queen, my love."

"But Maman is—"

Turning me so I'm straddling him now, he cups my chin with his large, warm hand. "To save you, she forfeited her right a century ago.

The magic within her, the aegis, no longer sees her as the owner, but a familial relation to the true heir."

"But what if it doesn't? She deserves to lead her people the way she never got the chance to."

"That's where you're wrong, and I hope the dream you walked through showed you just how much." Seeing the confused expression on my face, Leonardo kisses my nose and then lips in the softest of pecks before pulling back. "Your mother sacrificed everything to ensure that you could take the crown someday, Anaya. She loved her people so much, she gave them the greatest gift in you, and I'll be with you every step of the way. Your people will rise again with you as queen."

"But what about my role here? My relationship with you means more to me than any—"

"There's nothing you can't do, my little wonderous fae."

"You give me a lot of credit, Leo."

"And you've earned more than trust to do so."

"Okay. We figure this out together." My fangs drop at the endearment, my lips ready to devour his, but stop just as I embed my fingers in the back of his hair. "How did you know I 'dream walked,' as you call it? Why did that happen?"

"Because my parents have a way of showing their loved ones the way when all seems lost. Something in your reactions yesterday drew my mother's gift, and she guided your mind to see what you'd missed in the past. There was something in that memory that needed—"

"The amulet." There's no doubt in my mind. The way it glowed like Larue's ring.

"What amulet, Anaya?"

"I'll tell you when we get there." Lowering my face to his, I kiss my male with all the love, devotion, and my promise to never stop worshipping him. It's a little sloppy, and the tang of his blood mixed with his unique hint of chocolat causes an explosive frenzy inside of me. I want him—the slutty side of me he brings out by simply breathing is hungry for her mate—but now isn't the right time.

We have somewhere to be, and it isn't going to be a fun trip. Many hate me there.

Slowing the kiss, I rub our noses together and smile. "Come, King Moore. It's time I show you my kingdom."

"Good girl."

"YOU'RE NOT WELCOME HERE, TRAITOR." I hear his voice before I see him, the prior king's voice thundering across the throne room where all grievances are heard. This is one of three in the palace, the false king demanding to separate the commoners from the elite and this change was the start.

No longer a single fae court, but now segregated by monetary value. One more important than the other.

Yet this is the original.

My people's history is embedded into every wall. Into every golden pillar.

"An assumption no one asked you to make, Grand-Père. Although it's lovely to see another lackey doing his lord's dirty work." My voice is steady, not belying my nerves at seeing him. I need to test my theory, one my male is aware of and waiting in the shadows, to react if needed. He wanted to take charge and protect me, but I needed to stand on my own two feet.

Show them all I'm not scared anymore.

"You are a failure like your moth—" Grandfather shakes his head profusely then, hard from side to side.

"Go on. I'm a failure like who?"

"Amelia let everyone down when she...what the hell?"

I take a step closer, then another, not stopping until I'm inches from him. Well within arm's reach. "Hurts, doesn't it?"

He's blinking hard, shaky hands running down his face before realizing just how close I am. His features harden and his fangs drop, a clear sign of aggression.

"Why did it take you so long to find me? I've been waiting for three hours, even grabbed what I came for." From my pocket, I pull out a stone just like the one around his neck hanging from a thick, golden chain. It falls to just below mid-chest and is duller than I've ever seen it.

Just as cheap as the one in between my fingers.

"*Princesse, you're back!*" *A squeal calls my attention to a woman I've known all my life. The keeper of the best-spiced chocolat in the world, Chef Ninon is smiling at me, eyes flicking between me and the imposing male against my back. "Is he your...?"*

"*Nosy.*" *It's a playful admonishment, one she giggles at. You'd never know by looking at her that this fae female is well over nine hundred years old when her appearance is that of a gorgeous forty-year-old woman. "But yes. This is my mate, King Leonardo Moore."*

"*Your Highness,*" *she says with reverence, no malice or distrust. "Thank you for accepting our Anaya. She's an innocent in—*"

"*She is my world.*" *A simple sentence, but the meaning is deep. Honest. "My queen."*

"*Beautiful.*" *Ninon curtsies, a tradition I'm not the fondest of, but I understand it's done with respect. "Please let me design your binding cake. It'd be my greatest honor to."*

"*Thank you.*" *Without thinking twice, I hug the woman. She's been in my life—my mother's life—all these years and treated us as people and not commodities. "But I'm going to need something else from you. Can you help me?"*

"*Oui.*"

"*Then get me into Larue's office without detection. I don't want to be seen yet.*"

"I've already visited with our chef and a few maids, and even had words with the newly appointed general, and he recognized *my* authority at once. Pledged his allegiance to me." Tapping the worthless rock on my chin, I pretend to think. "Why is that, Grandfather? What's defective in you?"

"You've used dark magic! You're marked by that Wiccan—" He doesn't get to finish as my closed fist connects with his jaw. I have to jump a bit to do so, my height barely reaching his chest, but the impact has its desired effect. Grandfather swings to attack as my male puts him in a chokehold from behind and holds him still so I can yank that offending amulet off him.

It falls somewhere to our left, shattering upon impact, and Grand-Père's legs give out. He's wobbly, disoriented at once, and then passes out.

His labored breathing is the only sign of life left.

CHAPTER 12

Anaya

"They might win against me, ma princesse, but not you. You are stronger and fiercer than what you believe and will one day rule more than one kingdom with a male as pure-hearted as you."

That theory's been tested over the last week as my family arrived and the military from each kingdom took control of all entry points of the city. Vampires, Werewolf, and Wiccan guards have all descended upon my territory by invitation and are working with newly appointed General Francois and his men who are loyal to me.

All others have been dismissed from their charges. Outraged, those of a past, high-ranking status have hurled insults my way and spat at my feet but have been smart enough to do so from a distance. They won't come near me; to do so would be a sure death sentence. An elder learned that the hard way coming out of my grandfather's hospital room.

"Wiccan whore," he hissed at me, *eyes narrowed in disgust. "You've brought great shame to your people. Your father would be alive if it wasn't for the despicable family you've spread your legs for. I'd be doing the world a great service if I ended—"*

The old man never finished his sentence, and his entrails were later displayed outside the palace entrance, a clear message to all that this queen has a true king. Leonardo cut him open from his lower back to his neck with the use of a sword he'd taken a fancy to, and General Francois was all too happy to gift it to the Wiccan ruler two days after our arrival.

Mother's opal dagger sat embedded in the elder's skull until his body was carried out the back door, displaying the grotesque image for all to see. Only then, at the threshold, did my male remove the knife, brain matter dripping from the tip, and then smiled at the group of Larue sympathizers who watched.

Fear. Ire. Disgust.

They hated us, but always from afar. Not one is brave enough to come close and incur his wrath.

It also burns them how many have rejoiced over the end of a tyranny that should never have been. Those of a lower ranking have given me their heartfelt acceptance and pledged their loyalty, cursing the very existence of the man they still worship and revere as if still alive.

It's sickening how low some will fall to stay within a position of power because the coffer is large, but greedy are the hands. They will fight tooth and nail to subjugate their fellow man, no matter how wrong it is. No matter the pain inflicted upon innocent people who just want the right to live in peace and share a prosperity that benefits everyone.

The world would be a better place if people remembered that to give is to receive.

That good intentions and equality are the literal signs of prosperity.

"Would you like something to drink, Anaya?" Isabella asks from my right, pulling me from my thoughts, her hand in mine as we sit vigil inside my grandfather's room. He's been twitching all morning, groaning as the strange fever that held him captive for days finally breaks. "Are you hungry at all?"

"No. A little nauseous, to be honest." That causes a raised brow, maybe a bit of surprise in her expression, but that's it. Nothing else. I bump my shoulder with hers. "Don't think I didn't notice your lack of appetite either, Luna. You okay?"

"I will be. Just adjusting."

"The heartbeat is strong. My ears picked up on the difference as soon as you walked in the door." I'm watching her reaction from the corner of my eye and she grins, not hiding her happiness. "But I'm guessing no one else knows?"

"Not yet." A tiny giggle slips out of her, and she has to bite her bottom lip to get it under control. You're not supposed to be this happy in a hospital room with an unconscious family member inches away, but I laugh too. It's one of those "you start and I follow," only to do it all over again when you think you have it under control. *Such bad behavior.* It takes her a second, but she holds the glee long enough to pat her stomach and turn her head in my direction. Her blue eyes, so much like Leo's, swim with happiness. "Xadiel scented our pup the day before we came to see you. That's why we arrived so late. We made a tiny pitstop in England to announce it to our kingdom."

"I'm so happy for you. Aunt Aya is going to spoil the little alpha."

"Thank you." In a move so like Isa, she kisses my cheek and then turns serious. "Ask me."

"Will everyone else be okay? Are *you* okay to be in the middle of this mess?"

"Smart cookie." Isa leans her head against mine, and her open hand touches mine. "Things will get rough, sister of the heart, but I promise no harm will come to those who don't deserve it."

"That's a bit vague…"

"Seers usually are," Leonardo interrupts then, his sweaty arms lifting me from my seat so he can occupy the chair and place me on his lap. He's dressed for training. All three kings sparred today. "Quit worrying, Anaya. We will find her."

"I don't understand why we can't locate the building having the exact coordinates. Places just don't disappear, and my mother—"

"What's wrong with my daughter?" All three heads snap in his direction, finding my grandfather awake and very much alert for a man who's been comatose for days. "Tell me, Anaya. Where is my Amelia?"

To be honest, this is the part of the conversation I have no idea how to conduct. Silence ensues after his request; he watches me the same way I'm looking at him, with confusion—trying to decipher if he can trust me—and I'm at a loss. Years of conditioning and mistreatment have left me brimming with the need to strike out and lay every single sin at his feet, but *something* stops me.

Maybe it's because his eyes are clearer than I've ever seen them.

Maybe it's the desperation in his tone.

Maybe it's because he looks at the man whose lap I'm sitting on with recognition, not hatred, and that softens me. Not enough to lie, but enough to soften the blow as I detail every single moment of pain and mistreatment my mother endured at his hands. Under the fists of the man he worshipped like a God.

His bellows of pain fill the space with a cacophony of *no's* and *oh Gods, my Mellie*; his pain is palpable, and yet I still walk out of the room. While he cries and asks my mate questions, I send him a mental message to *Stay*. For now, I just need fresh air. To have my earned moment of tears, because come tomorrow, I will find my mother.

This fight has just begun, and Silla has no idea the enemy she made out of me.

The former king is the key to finding Queen Amelia, but it'll be my hands that end the spiteful, bitter witch who destroyed our lives. And like Wiccans vow, I, too, whisper…

"So mote it be."

"WILL you ever see me without scorn inside your heart?" My grandfather stops beside me, his hand on the balcony's railing. We've just received word of an unrest deep into the city's center led by what's left of Brice's battalion. Seems he's been in contact with men who've been dismissed from duty after refusing to address me correctly.

I'm no one's concubine, much less a belonging. His men don't see it that way and have gone into hiding, coming out like little children to cast a stone and then run, pretending they have no clue how the porcelain China broke.

They're accosting those who side with me. Burning small businesses and beating lone guards they catch off shift. The bright side in all this? I've given all military occupying the territory free reign to incarcerate, no matter the social ranking, those who hurt others. Especially the defenseless.

Violence will not be permitted. Enough is enough.

"It will take some time, but yes. I think someday I will." It's the truth. In the forty-eight hours since waking up, he's been open with me. Communicating and helping the werewolf luna scribe for my mother's location and each time, they've come out with empty hands. We've had people fly over the location and drive to it, but all they find are vast trees and an open lake with no building in sight.

It's not right. None of this is.

"It was not me, Anaya. That asshole," he spits out with so much venom my eyes snap to his—his amethyst eyes open and in so much pain—and my eyes become blurry with unshed tears. "That ungrateful bastard and his sister have robbed me of everything, ma joie. I didn't get to see my only child grow into her role as queen and find true happiness, teaching her daughter our ways. I didn't get to see you grow up and blossom, meet your mate, and then witness your bonding ceremony in front of both kingdoms."

That makes me blush a bit. "We haven't done that yet."

His brows furrow. "What do you mean? You've marked him and—"

"We want Silla and her daughter dead first. That, and my mother home where she belongs... she's been away long enough."

"I'm so sorry, my child. I've let you down, and it pains me to have done so. You both deserved more from me."

The sincerity in his voice melts a bit of my resentment away, allowing my heart to be a little more rational. Glamoured individuals are puppets, and for a century, the former king was a *yes* man and nothing more.

"You think so?"

"I know so." Conviction. Honesty.

Take this olive branch. Please don't let me down.

"Then prove it, Grand-Père. Please, help me find your daughter."

THE CAR STOPS about twenty yards from the geographical location on the map we brought with us from Leo's coven. It's quiet and it should feel breezy with how the trees sway, but all I feel is cold.

Barren and desolate coldness. The kind that seeps into your bones and leaves you aching for hours unless you bundle up and hide under a blanket. Then, there's the lack of animal noises, especially as we watch what looks like pigeons circulate the top of an awkward treetop, the top misshapen into a pointed incline, and I tilt my head to the side.

"Too many oddities."

"Agreed." Grandfather takes a step forward, and then another, abandoning the area where we parked and studying. A particular spot near the bottom left of a gnarled tree trunk. *Glitching* would be the best way to describe it, fluctuating between a solid mass and an opaqueness in tones that are not normal. Especially not in nature. "You're seeing that, right?"

"I see it, Luca," Leonardo answers, his arm around my waist pulling me back into step with him. That was his only rule; I'm never to be out of his arm's reach no matter what. My safety is his priority. "You think they glamoured this place, too? How are they managing the amount of magic needed to keep this illusion running?"

"That might be the scariest answer we find." Bending at the waist, I find a no-bigger-than-a-fist-sized rock and hand it to Leo. "Can you toss it right at the edge, between the wood and the figurine of a squirrel?" My male does so and the entire thing freezes, showing a broken opening where there was none, and I catch sight of yellow. Bright yellow. "Do it again? Maybe with something bigger this—"

I'm stopped by Grandfather's hand lifting, a calmness about him that exudes out, and what looks like a hundred pebbles concentrate on the spot Leo weakened. Simultaneously, they ping and prod and force open a hole big enough to walk through as the illusion splinters around the bottom edge, but it doesn't shatter.

The rest stays in place; its magic is strong, and I'm thankful for it as we draw near and catch two voices. Both female.

Both have been on the run long enough.

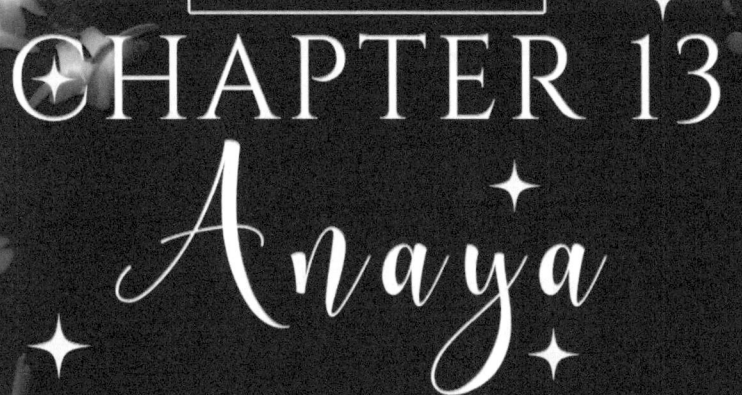

CHAPTER 13

Anaya

"This is getting out of hand, Lady Chiara. We're going to get caught."

"Quit worrying. Mother secured these grounds herself after that idiot Larue got himself killed." There's so much glee in Chiara's voice, and the little squeal that follows makes me sick to my stomach, something that causes me to rub the area. Leo catches sight of it and watches me for a moment, but there's no heartbeat yet. Even if my first bleed after mating hasn't arrived, a normal occurrence for any newly mated female, it doesn't mean I am with child.

Right now, I'm just a bag of nerves and nothing more. So close to seeing my mother again.

Did he hear or scent something I haven't, though?

"If Silla continues to bleed Amelia and those poor rejected women at the rate she's going, it will all crash." That stops my train of thought, and I concentrate on the two women speaking freely on the other side of the door. They don't sense us. "This kind of magic can only hold for so long without feeding; you know it's becoming more demanding each day. We're losing three donors every week."

"Brice is working on a solution, Lena. Have you lost all faith in the cause?"

"Is Silla okay with him stepping in and—"

"What Mother doesn't know won't hurt her." Chiara's tone cuts off any further discussion, not that it matters because *I* lose what's left of my control.

All my life, I've been a healer. A woman who loves and gives and can't stand the thought of someone being in pain when I can step in and take it as my own, helping their bodies mend faster than any medicine our hospitals can provide.

I healed Roberto numerous times when Silla's play left him half-dead, much to her shock.

I took care of Maman even when she demanded I stop. That I protect myself.

Maids and new guards and anyone that the elders hurt, I gave them a little of me to alleviate the aches and pains that came from serving the fake king and his pathetic court.

But this time—this time, I deliver the pain.

Raw furry erupts and before Leo can stop me, I'm slamming the unlocked front door wide open, ignoring the heinous bronze knocker and landing a punch straight onto Chiara's face. Blood splatters seconds after impact, coating my face and shirt while the banshee beneath me screams in agony.

Her nose is broken, and I hit her there again and again until the skin breaks and a fragment of cartilage hangs loose from the opening. I give her everything in me: the pent-up rage and agonizing pain I've felt these years.

The need to avenge all the lives lost. The rejected innocents who had their chance at a second love pairing stolen from them.

From elbows to punches—scratches that leave gouges on her cheeks before I'm pulled off by a pair of strong hands. I'm tucked against a strong chest as the scent of chocolate and cloves brings me down from a plane of ire I've never experienced before.

The people they've hurt...

I turn in Leonardo's arms, ready to launch myself on her again, but what I find is a horrified Lena and an unconscious Chiara, the latter of which has been beaten to the point of rapid facial swelling and a spreading puddle of blood beneath her head.

She's alive, her chest rising and falling, and I find myself feeling no remorse for what I've done.

The bitch deserves it and more.

"You—" Whatever Lena was going to say dies on her evil tongue when my head snaps in her direction. Instead, she shifts closer to my grandfather, who looks down at her kneeling form in disgust.

"Take me to her."

"I can't. There's no—"

"You are in no position to speak, but since you prefer things to be done the hard way, I'll appease you, old witch." Leonardo's tone reverberates throughout the foyer, the same place they ambushed my mother and me all those years ago, and he unleashes an animalistic growl full of command—the decree of a king to his subject. "You will stand, lower your head, and take us to Amelia without uttering a single word. Understood?" The witch nods and he adds power to the command, the weight almost too heavy for her, and her knees shake. "Now. Move it."

Without the ability to fight it, Lena turns and we walk deeper into the house and toward a small door in the kitchen. It's locked. The thick metal has a combination sequence she doesn't know, but that doesn't stop my male.

He rips the door off its hinges, tossing the thick wood toward the hallway while my grandfather carries a still-passed-out Chiara in his arms down the stairs.

This was Grand-Père's stipulation after asking for his help. He goes first, saving me from what could be worse than never-knowing.

Because speculations still hold a glimmer of hope, while raw evidence robs you of possibilities for a happier future.

"Clear." One word, and I move to rush down the steps, but Leo doesn't allow it. After pointing at the old witch to walk down, I'm swept up in his arms and carried until we reach the cold basement floor.

Goddess. I'm struck speechless.

"My poor child. My people." Grandpa drops Chiara and her body bounces, the concrete not the friendliest of surfaces, and another split in her skin appears.

She no longer has a healthy glow. Instead, she's bruised and bleeding, just like the four women inside the room.

Yet it's the one at the center with a dirty drip embedded into the crook of her elbow via a large needle that I'm focusing on. While my mate starts to release the weakened woman, tears roll down my eyes as a shocked sob leaves me. Her face is pallid and her eyes sunken in, but Queen Amelia's beauty can never be dulled.

She still smells of lilies and home, of moments spent outside in her garden as a young child helping her plant those fragrant blooms. Of kisses on the cheek for a job well done and stories in her bed when she grew too weak to stand.

All this time, they'd been tearing her apart, but this…

"Maman," I whisper low, my steps rushing to her as her father releases her feet first and then hands from her bindings, being careful not to further injure her.

The needle comes out next and she grimaces, eyes slowly opening just enough to see me, and then whispers a five-word greeting.

"Anaya, my brilliant little queen."

"I'm here." My palms begin to glow as my gift rises to the

surface, and I place them on either side of her head. I'm feeding her enough of my essence to transport her out of here, something Leo worries about—his concern causing me to pull back as Mother's cheeks becomes less gaunt and her eyes snap wide open.

And once I know she's secure, it's my turn to pass out. The second heartbeat picks this moment to make his presence known—strong and demanding it so.

WHEN I COME TO, I'm inside of Wiccan territory with my mother lying in a hospital bed to my right, her face watching me in wonder. Tears form in her violet orbs and mine simultaneously, the pain of being robbed of so much precious time crushing, but then I remember something else.

My hands instinctively cover my abdomen moments before Leonardo rushes inside. He looks tired as his eyes meet mine, the dark circles beneath them showing his exhaustion. "How long was I out? Is the baby—"

"Our little one is safe and happy inside his perfect mother," he croons once beside me, his large hands cupping my face as he lowers his to mine. And the smile that greets me as soon as we're exchanging breaths is pure magic. His mere presence rights any wrong committed against me, because at the end of my journey, I have everything. His love, our home, and now a little one who will grow up with the previous generations of faes to coddle and dote on the tiny monarch. Just like his father, uncles, and aunts will teach him about other species and how special our family is. *Perfectly chaotic, but a perfect blend.* "I'm the happiest man on earth, my precious one. This blessing is a gift from the Gods after so much suffering. He or she will be the best part of us; a fae witch hybrid with the heart of a warrior for his people. Both of them."

"Leonora always said you two would make a cute couple," Maman interjects, and our faces turn in her direction; her hands are intertwined against her chest while a big smile spreads across her face. "And I must say that sly witch was right. But then again, she constantly cheated, Paolo's gift making it all the easier for her."

Leo snorts while picking me up gently and then slipping in beneath me. He places me on his lap while running blunt fingernails down my hair, the action so soothing. "My father had no shame when it came to his mate. None."

"Like father, like son, then?"

"Guilty." Leo looks down at me, and I skim my fingertips across the dark circles, healing a bit of his exhaustion, which earns me a harsh nip to my finger. "Don't. You need your energy."

"I didn't even feel that."

"She's always been a stubborn one, Leonardo. That's never going to change, it seems." It's not admonishing, more like pride in her voice. From my sideways position on my male's lap, I watch her wipe away a few stray tears as they fall. "He didn't break my baby, and for that, I'm eternally grateful. She's still just as pure-hearted and kind as the day she was born."

"And how are *you* feeling, Maman?"

My mother takes in a deep breath and lets it out slowly, her smile dropping a bit. More of a grimace now. "Mostly tired, and still not fully convinced this isn't just another dream, but if it is, I don't want to wake up. Leaving you behind, and not fighting harder to stay by your side, will always be my greatest regret, Aya. I should've had Ninon take you out of the city and hide you from Larue, but my fear of the worst coming to fruition held me back. And now, after years of living with that pain, one of my tormentors is asking for forgiveness while my innocent daughter looks at me with love, not hate—and it's overwhelming. I'm a little lost."

"Then it's a good thing you have all the time in the world to heal and make peace, Amelia. There's no rush to leave my lands or an expiration date on absolving your father of the sins committed under a heavy glamor." Leonardo's stare is honest as he conveys what could be viewed as a command but done so out of love. No malice.

There is no ulterior motive. "You, yourself, were a victim of that crime, so take your time and heal. Rest, eat…gather your strength, because my little queen needs you and so does our babe."

"I think some time alone to gather your thoughts will help, Maman. You've spent so much time as a prisoner that you have no idea what you want." Reluctantly, she nods at my assessment. "Why don't you spend the next few days in this room resting? We'll bring everything you could need up here, and I will come and visit in the evenings to reconnect. Slowly. Giving us a chance to catch our breaths while assimilating to this new reality."

"I'd like that. I don't want to be without you again."

"You won't be." Tapping Leo's thigh, I shift my head in her direction. *Take me to her, my love. I'm going to hug her before we leave.* In one swift move, he does as I ask, and I'm able to wrap my arms around my mother's neck and kiss her forehead as she silently weeps in my hold. Her tears wet my top while mine fall, but I pay no mind to where they land, and she whispers low apologies over things that were never under her control.

Those responsible will pay.

For her. For me. For my unborn child.

They will never separate us again.

CHAPTER 14
LEONARDO

I'd like to put in a grievance to my male's complaint department.

I've been lied to. There is no naughty fae list!

My king has failed to back up his threat, and I'm left wondering...

Did that punishment list vanish somehow? Did it ever truly exist?

Forever Yours,
Anaya

"**I**s it comfortable? Can you see anything?" I ask Anaya, tweaking the satin sash covering her eyes, making sure the knot at the back is comfortable. The last thing I want is another headache for her; she's been battling one on and off over the last few days, and while she claims it's normal after using her healing ability, I'd rather not take any chances.

Moreover, I want today to be perfect. I want to spoil my little fae queen while pushing away our responsibilities, family problems, and the prisoner demanding her release after awakening in one of my heavily silvered confinement cells.

To Chiara's detriment, I couldn't give a rat's ass over her displeasure or the need for a hot shower. Prison cells are meant to be uncomfortable; they're not a spacious retreat. This isn't a vacation destination with an all-inclusive buffet or liquor as an attraction amenity.

Her screams have fallen on no one's ears as outside of meals, it's just her and Lena. I haven't visited or talked to either woman. *Let them stew.*

"I'm feeling great, Leonardo. So excited."

"Do you trust me?" My nose twitches then as her scent thickens, sugary sweet with her arousal, and my chest rumbles in response. The sound is not quite a purr, but since finding out she's pregnant with my first little one, I find myself humming for her, a deep vibration she responds to with a cute whine—a needy sound that settles and then converts into a content moan.

It's the cutest fucking thing. Something I look forward to for the length of this pregnancy, and the next, more so when I think about her round and waddling around the house. The future nights in our bed, my hand splayed over her stomach as our child pushes against her confinement chamber and I rub the area to settle her or him down.

I'm surprised Isabella hasn't called to congratulate us.

For the time being, we're playing the waiting game. Each sibling has gone home, but our armies have stayed in France to monitor the area. We want to know who comes in and out of the fae court. Who they congregate with, and more importantly, how many of the elders are involved in the minor acts of rebellion that have risen across the city since Larue's death.

"To the ends of the earth and back." No hesitation. Her trust in me is humbling, but more than that, it's sexy as fuck. Something I treasure and will use against her as I collect a debt owed.

Her sassy note is responsible for our date. The location was also inspired by it.

Guiding her by the small of her back, I walk us to the circular driveway where one of my horses already awaits. He's saddled, and there's a plush blanket ready for me to bundle her up in while she enjoys the slow ride from my lap. We're not going far.

It'll be a slow gait; I plan to keep her in a heightened state of curiosity without being able to see where we are or where we're going. Stopping before the horse, I take her hand in mine and rub across my prized Salernitano, petting his nose in slow, downward strokes that pull a giggle from her.

While Onyx and Pearl stayed with Isabella and are retired now, I followed tradition and bought two myself. Our father loved this breed. So did our mother. They're strong, can withstand enchantments, and have life expectancies that reach well over ninety, with some animals living far longer.

They can also travel for long stretches without the need to rest.

Loving and loyal; the honey-colored guy Aya's petting now is the younger of my two.

"This is Atlas." My front is pressed to her back, body curving over her much smaller frame. "He's going to take us on a little trip. You ready?"

"Am I allowed to take the blindfold off to get the full experience?"

"No." I chuckle at her grumpy huff. "Behave, little fae. We're not going too far. Just sit back and enjoy."

"Sit where?" Her tone is a bit suggestive, and it takes everything in me to not empale her on my cock now, but there's a time and place for everything. With all the craziness of the last few weeks: her family reuniting, our search for Silla—the small changes that come with a new pregnancy—our alone time has been limited to stolen moments and quick rides before a knock comes to our door.

Something she bemoans. Something I loathe.

As a newly mated pair, we should've taken some time off to connect and enjoy and explore, but we also understand that the situation is beyond us. That we're being blessed by the Gods and treat every moment as such.

I'll just have to steal her away more often to compensate.

Move two steps back. I got you. That gives me just enough room to mount my horse and still have her within reach to lift and place sidesaddle with the blanket on her lap before taking off. Atlas is trained to follow clicks; three of them indicate a slow and steady gait, his movements barely jostling us as we weave through the trees behind our home.

The path leading us toward my surprise is just a few feet away, and Atlas shifts onto the narrow cobblestone street with ease. It's a straight shot from here, a secluded, man-made wading pool I designed and carved myself as a mating present for my future intended.

It's a project that kept me busy during years when the loneliness hit me hard.

My parents were dead.

Isabella was busy keeping our futures secure.

Gabriella was dead, and reborn a century after marrying her vampire.

During that time, all I had was Silla. She raised me, which is why I can never forgive her crimes.

Breaking through the trees, we come to a stop at the edge of a raised platform where a mattress, plush blankets, and more pillows than are needed await us. There's a cooler with ice and our preferred drinks, and a basket packed with caprese sandwiches, prosciutto and melon skewers, pasta salad, and an entire tiramisu to share.

I have candles and massage oils.

Towels to dry off if she decides to cool off or float in the clear water.

"I'm going to lower you now. Stay calm."

"Okay. Ready." Dismounting her is quick and I jump off quickly after, sweeping my sweet little gift off her feet and climbing onto the bedding. Only then, when she's sitting between my thighs and biting her bottom lip in excitement, do I remove the blindfold.

I wait.

And wait some more.

Anaya's gone speechless as she twists her head from side to side, taking in the most minute detail I've prepared for this date, from each cushion, to the fabric beneath our bodies, and then the delicate baskets used to transport our lunch. She *oohs* and *ahhs* over all of it, but the real excitement comes in the form of a squeal when our private oasis becomes her focus.

The pool itself is carved five feet deep and in an oval shape with the edges made out of smoothed-out travertine. The opulent stone slopes and then disappears beneath the crystal-clear water, adding to the natural beauty of the shimmering surface.

There's a solar-powered water feature.

A flat area to sunbathe.

And what's better, no one is allowed on this section of my property. We will not be interrupted.

"This is beautiful, Leonardo. How did you find this place?"

"I didn't." My answer causes her brows to furrow, but before she can ask, I continue. "I built this, Anaya. Everything here was dug, carved, polished, and connected by me."

"How long did it take you to create this? It had to be before I moved here."

Lying back on the mattress, I kick off my shoes and pull her down with me. Turn us so we're side by side, facing each other. *Goddess, she's beautiful.* "I started working on this place over a decade ago and added things to it slowly. Always thinking about what my queen would like, adding touches of comfort to please her." Leaning over, I press my lips to hers. Just hold them there. "I was never actively searching for a mate, Anaya, but I'm blessed to call you mine. The Gods rewarded my patience. They gave me the greatest gift and lesson the moment our eyes met."

"Why a lesson?"

"Because for so long, I thought of and wanted nothing more than to kill your father. Avenging my parents was my sole purpose in life."

And now?"

"Now I have you, and you supersede everything. Everyone."

"You, me, and our baby."

"Team Moore for life," I say, and she giggles, but that soon turns into a yawn. Another difference in her; she's been needing naps in the middle of the day for the last week. Isotta and Annette assured me it was normal; pregnant women go through different needs for the duration, and being a little extra tired is all part of the gig.

"Sleep, sweetheart. I'll watch over you."

"Maybe you can nap with me instead?" Begging violet eyes, a soft smile, and the cute way she pats her stomach—I can't say no. Tugging the blanket free from beneath me, I cover us before whispering a low incantation meant to protect the area and my family while we rest.

Neve laedat hoc sacrum spatium.
Neve laedat hoc sacrum spatium.
Neve laedat hoc sacrum spatium.

WARM. Wet. Heat.

I'm pulled from sleep by the pleasure enveloping my cock, the pulses rushing through me from my head to my balls, and then it spreads through every limb of my body. It feels so good, more so when an electrical pulse shocks me right where my mating mark sits.

"Bad little fae." My voice is rough from sleep as I open my eyes to the most beautiful sight in the world: Anaya licking me from base to tip—paying special attention to my mating mark—as if I were a melting ice cream. Her tiny tongue is worshipping every ridge and vein, adding pressure on the underside and then drawing down to my balls where she suckles the right one into her mouth before moving to the left. "Fuck, Anaya. That mouth of yours is heaven."

"Is it?" she asks, languid in her movement. No hurry as she gives a tiny nip with her fangs to the base of my cock, causing me to jump. I like the sting. Enjoy the pain. "This also doesn't feel like a punishment. You lied, and that list was an imaginary threat all along..."

"Anaya."

"Yes, Leonardo?"

"Run." Violet eyes flash with heat as she lands a second bite above the first and then takes off, a little blood on her lips. Because she's pregnant, I won't tackle her and fuck an imprint of her perky ass into the ground, but there are other ways to win.

Her footfalls light on the grass, she heads toward the water feature and pauses when she's on the other side. As if my being on one side of the pool and her on the other is enough to keep me at bay. *She wants to get caught.* "That's not running, precious one."

"I'm simply being fair and allowing you a moment to get close before I slip away."

"Is that so?"

"Yes."

It takes no effort from me to run and jump across the pool, landing beside her. However, as my hand skims her neck to grasp it,

Anaya runs. She really pumps those lithe legs this time, and I throw my head back in laughter as she zips through the trees in the direction we came.

I count from one to twenty in my head, the head start enough for her to reach Atlas who rests near a feeding post. His head snaps up when she runs past him, a little confused, but he goes right back to relaxing when I follow her a few seconds later.

The warlock in me is excited. Both the human side and the magic want to dominate this creature. We want her on her knees again. Want to have her litter my cock with bites and licks before I kiss the back of her throat.

Up ahead, she takes a turn and I bite my bottom lip, deviating from her trail. To the left of me, there's a small unused cave, but beyond that, it merges with the path she's on as it becomes a looping circle back to the way she came. Most of the paths here all lead back. It's why I chose this area to build my gift.

You can't get lost when all roads lead to the beginning.

In time, I'll teach her which one to take back home, but for now, I'm not above using this to my advantage. She comes around the bend and hasn't seen me yet. Anaya's looking back over her shoulder when I step into her path. In seconds, she is within my reach. On her next intake of breath, I have her off the ground and yelping, whirling her head back to me with those perfect lips making an *O*.

"What the? How?"

My response is a quick spank to her ass as I carry her back to the pool. She's squirming in my hold and fights me to get down, but my grip doesn't lessen. If anything, the hand on her thigh tightens as I carry her back past the platform and straight to the travertine edge of the pool.

Only then do I allow her feet to touch the ground.

Only then do I speak.

"Turn around and bend over, hands on your ankles."

CHAPTER 15
Anaya

"*Turn around and bend over, hands on your ankles.*"

Excitement and desire rush through me, nearly taking my breath at the command. My body's thrumming with excitement, my thighs slick with my arousal, and I'm not ashamed to have taunted him into giving me what I need.

His surprise was too sweet. The surrounding area is lush and the accommodations in our oasis are straight out of a magazine, but I need more.

To reconnect.

To feel owned.

Licking my lips, I drag my tongue slowly over the dried specs of his blood, and bend. I've always been flexible, and I'm grateful for that gift now as I go the extra mile and place my palms flat on the ground while spreading my thighs wide.

My holes are exposed to him, the cool breeze and his following groan only making me slicker.

My arousal drips out of my entrance; I feel the rush as it coats my lips and then rolls down and onto the polished stone.

"Prettiest fucking cunt. So pink and wet." I hear a guttural groan seconds before he cups me from behind. Just holds me while spreading my juices before slipping two fingers inside. "So tight, and *motherfuck*, precious one. You're clenching so hard. This needy little pussy is begging to be fucked."

"Please." I try to push back on his fingers, to set the pace, but it only earns me a strike across my right asscheek. "Oh!"

Fire blooms and spreads where he spanked, and it feels so *good.*

"That first one is for being bratty." Leonardo's voice is deeper, a near snarl a second before I receive a second smack, this time to the area just above where my asscheek and thigh meet. *Goddess help me.* "This one is for that smart mouth. You should be sucking my cock, not anticipating the next smack."

My fangs drop, and a full-body shiver rolls through me at his command. Because that's what it is: my sole job is to please him.

I'm trying to figure out the logistics of how to stay bent over while taking him in my mouth when I'm suddenly airborne and placed over his body.

Leonardo maneuvers us so he's on his back and I'm straddling his chest with easy access to his cock.

The tip glistens with beads of pre-come that roll down his shaft as it throbs inches from my face.

"Leo!" He lands the third smack right at the cleft, fingers grazing both of my clenching holes. I'm so wet, and he sees everything in this position.

His broad chest forces me to spread wide, my knees barely touching the ground, and it feels more like I'm suspended for his amusement. His pleasure.

"That's for not wrapping your lips around my cock the moment I gifted you access." Two fingers run from my pussy to rosebud, dragging my slick and spreading it. He wipes it on my skin too, as if it were paint and he was creating a masterpiece with my arousal.

"So you're making up punishments now? That's not on the list." My small hand wraps around his thickness, fingers barely touching, as I pump him slowly. I'm mesmerized by the pearl-like drops as they gather and roll down until…

"Fuck, baby, bite a little deeper." Another demand. But since that first night together, I've noticed his desire to feel my fangs. To lick them. To have them break his skin. "Gods, that's it. Use that little tongue to catch every drop."

I don't retract my teeth from his tip, but suckle as I am. I'm lapping his blood and pre-come, letting it slide down my tongue as the rest of me heats and my ass arches for his touch.

I'm rewarded by two thick fingers sliding in and a firmer smack right over the curve of my left side. For some reason, this one hurt a little more, but the intense feeling after sending electrical pulses to my clit and I cry out, flooding his fingers buried deep. He hits the same spot again and again, fire spreading through the area as I ride his fingers and retract my bite, sliding him into my mouth, and I don't stop until reaching halfway.

I hold him there and swallow, letting my saliva drip down to his base and coat him before pulling off. Faes are sexual beings by nature. We enjoy and explore and aren't held back by insignificant things like gag reflexes or pain; we welcome it.

Our instincts guide us.

We take what our bodies demand.

And I've never felt freer in my life than splayed atop my mate, the only person who will ever see me at my most debased, with his cock resting on my tongue.

Every problem. Every bit of hurt.

The worrying…

It all fades, and all I see and hear is him. My savior.

"This one is for denying me your attention, Anaya. For letting someone of no significance into our space." Leonardo rains down five sharp smacks in alternating locations. "No one comes before you or me, unless it's our children who have an emergency. What we have is special, sweetheart. What I hoped my mating would someday be, and I'll protect it just as fiercely."

The pain strikes first and I whimper, sucking softly on his tip for comfort, when he changes fingers and claims both my holes, his thumb in one and two fingers in my pussy. It's different and good, and I once again take him deeper as a reward. He shivers beneath me and I smile, which he feels, and I'm taught a quick lesson in cockiness.

His long arm catches the ends of my hair and tugs enough that it stings. I arch up, and he finger fucks me until I'm shaking.

I'm trying to roll my hips but can't. I'm trying to get just a little more…that's all I need, but he stops and allows me to fall forward.

"Please!"

"Suck my cock, Anaya. I want to make a mess of that pretty face." His fingers in my pussy change their angle, the movement more precise, and I feel pressure. Each thrust digs deeper, his rhythmic movement focused on a specific spot inside of me, the pressure building in the front walls of my pussy. *Goddess,* I feel a rush of volcanic pleasure roll through me—unlike anything I've ever felt before—and my body responds with hunger.

For him. For his cock. Leonardo's pleasure becomes my sole focus at this moment.

His come on my tongue is my greatest desire. So much so, that I can almost taste it.

My every nerve ending is on fire. My wetness coats us both while my spit dribbles onto his head; we are a perfect mess. The physical manifestation of my desire for him—the way he can play with my body—drives him to thrust his fingers deeper. Faster.

The sounds and splatter of my slick are the perfect symphony to my pleasure. It mingles with my moans, creating the perfect note, but it's his male grunt that destroys me. I come on his fingers, lips parted over the crown of his length, the scream caught in my throat, and one he breaks through when I take him from tip to base down my throat.

"Such a good girl for her male. My pretty mate." His praise between my hungry whimpers is loud, and I'm thankful to be away from everyone for this private moment. There's simply no way I can hold back. I bob my head up and down while his hips below me piston, slowly at first, until I stop long enough to bite him again.

One to his thick base. One on his inner thigh, the latter of which earns me another spank.

"Don't be gentle, Leonardo. My king, I need this." Opening wide, I run my tongue down the underside, collecting his blood before taking the first few inches. Gripping his thighs, I dig my nails in, tearing through the dermis while taking him just far enough his head kisses the back of my throat, and the slower he is to meet my strokes, the more I break skin until he understands.

In our bed, there will be a time for gentle and sweet, but this isn't it.

He fucks my mouth without pause.

My male takes his pleasure while shifting the soaked-in-me fingers from my pussy to my rosebud and begins to force his way in. Not because he wants to hurt me—I find that a little pain is a beautiful thing when there's trust—but because I'm small and tight.

He works them in with steady pressure, every once in a while stopping to spread them and then pump his digits in deeper until bottoming out. Ecstasy. Between the gurgling sounds of him owning my throat, pumping his full length into my throat, and the slight burn in my derrière:

I do something I didn't know was possible.

This orgasm is different and unexpected, and I lose control of my lower half, soaking his chest. I'm shaking and my core is clenching, and if I've reached his face; I have no clue. Not that I care, either. I'm too busy swallowing every drop of his come when he bellows my name a few seconds later.

CHAPTER 16

Anaya

Something can be said for the basic lack of filter and decorum after a release so intense that you take a nap immediately after. There was no rousing me from sleep or feeding me, and I give the culprit to my predicament a stinky-eyed face like the ones in my sticker box.

There aren't that many in the package to begin with. My guess is the company wanted to focus more on the *happy* stickers and not so much on the grumpy ones, but the expression works after being left a shaky, messy, sleepy lump of fae.

That was hours ago, and it's *still* all his fault. Not on me at all.

"I love private picnics, Leonardo. I will retract my complaint now."

He stops carrying me then. Just pauses and looks down at me with the smuggest grin on his face. *Keep looking at me like that, Leo. I'll bite you again.* "I'll wear them with pride, my love."

"Stop it. Behave."

"Do you really want me to?" he asks, brow cocked.

"No. Negative. Never." No pause. No hesitation. Maybe I answered a little too fast and I might be blushing a bit, but I'm not called out on it. Instead, he bites back his laugh. *Such a good male.* "But seriously, I am tired and happy and ready for a third nap."

"Then let's get you to bed." Clearing my throat, I bring a hand up to his face before he starts walking. He lets me cup his cheek for a few seconds, five at the most, before turning his head and nuzzling my palm. Places a chaste kiss at the center. "I love you, Anaya."

"That's cheating." It leaves me a little breathy. A slight whine at the end. "I love you, too."

"All's fair."

"You suck." And before he can respond, because I'm aware I did just say that, I place a finger over his lips. There's something I want him to hear. "Leonardo Moore, I need you to understand that I never doubted you. Not for one second."

He licks my finger and then nudges it away with his chin. "But you didn't come to me either. We are a team, my heart. Your burdens are mine, too."

"I'm beginning to understand that." It's the complete truth. He's shown me as much through every obstacle we've faced so far. "I'm sorry, my male."

"Nothing for me to forgive. Just let me take care of you."

"I'm all yours." That declaration earns me a sweet kiss on the lips before we continue the walk home. Atlas is trotting up ahead, happy and leading the way back onto the property, but when he heads to what I now realize is a stable and not a storage building, Leo walks toward our home.

People greet us as we pass them, many stopping to hold our hand for a moment. It's a practice he started when young, and after seeing him do it unconsciously a few times, I asked him about it when I first arrived.

"My people have been through so much, precious one. They lost their king and queen, my sisters, and all they had left was me—a child. Thirteen summers just isn't a lot of living, I had no idea what I was doing, but I gave them what I could. Holding a witch's hand or placing my forehead against a guard birthed a connection to me. To the monarchs of the past and the future, I vowed on my life to protect." Leonardo's expression is soft. One I only ever see around me. *"The simple act gave them peace in a world where Wiccans were being hunted and our enemies were closer than we ever thought."*

"Don't they look cozy?" His words snap me out of the memory, and I turn my attention toward the area he's pointing to. More specifically, the people sitting there.

My maman and Uncle Roberto are sitting on a bench, side by side, and smiling. She's talking, and he's nodding while a group of children squeal past on their way to an evening lesson. They look at ease, not stressed or with an uncomfortable expression on either of their faces, and the sight soothes my soul for different reasons.

With my king, it's all-consuming and passion and tenderness.

With them, it's happiness because I love them both, each in their own way, and I want nothing more than to see them given a second chance. A real chance at love, even if it's not with each other.

I'VE FELT eyes on me all afternoon as the children of the Moore coven show me the new spell learned today. The young ones have been out playing in the fields all morning, learning how to plant blooms of every kind—something I did with my mother at that age— which they help grow with a small incantation and the nurturing of each seedling.

They're so adorable.

Jumping and chasing each other while little tendrils of magic fill the air. Each ribbon of color surrounds me; their excitement is so palpable I can almost touch it. They make me giggle. I'm laughing and down on my knees, hands covered in dirt as I cover each new flower so it can grow wild and free.

This is what a childhood should be. Full of wonder.

So bright and happy, full of excitement as each performs for me, except a little girl who blushes. She's the smallest of the group, her voice like a timid chime whenever she speaks.

"Are you not ready, Alice?" I ask, keeping my voice soft so as to not draw attention her way. The other children are busy commanding a small grouping of lilies they're growing as a gift to me. Next, they want to add sunflowers. "You don't have to—"

"Queen Anaya, who's that?" She points to the left of us and toward a giant tree where a man watches. He's leaning against the trunk casually, unbothered, and every muscle in my body tenses when his smirk widens.

Brice stands without a shirt and his wings are spread, scraping against the forest floor. He's angry at me, the malice in his eyes and aura almost making me cower back, but I stand my ground. *I'm not alone anymore.*

A clear challenge he accepts by crooking a single finger at me before taking off into the sky, and what's worse, he's wearing my father's ring.

The one given to our new king.

How did he get that?

That piece of jewelry has been lost since my father's death, left behind within the mess of his massacred body, and I'm certain there were no survivors to claim it, either.

That compound inside the Canadian territory was isolated; Larue was not one for neighbors and he would've bought off every landowner within a fifteen-mile radius to avoid trespassers.

My father was an egomaniac: a narcissistic and paranoid man afraid of his own shadow. He didn't trust guards or keep them on rotation long enough to build a rapport; to him, all were dispensable unless you belonged to his closed-off inner circle.

His son is dead.

Brice was arrested at the time.

All bodyguards are ripped apart.

Yet it's the general that remains, and he has a hidden card up his sleeve.

"Chiara." **Leonardo, bring patrols and get the children out of the forest. Brice ambushed me, and he's flying us up.**

"What did you say, ma princesse?" Brice asks as a roar fills the mental link between my male and me, and Leonardo is angry. *Don't go up. Wait for me.*

Brice hovers a few feet above me again, watching me, and I can't make the mistake of being distracted again. He's too close for comfort, and I didn't even hear him descend; I have the children to protect.

Alice whimpers, and I make a huge mistake when my eyes shift in her direction. One he takes advantage of, because before I can place myself in front of the huddled children, he swoops down and grabs the little girl before disappearing within the clouds, and the only map I have to find him is her frightened screams.

"Gods!" I hiss out, ignoring Leo's demand that I wait for him. These few minutes could be the difference between saving Alice, and Brice taking an innocent's life to get to me.

I can't allow that.

Yelling comes through our link as he tells Augusto to lock the cell doors and gather guards, to bring them to the panting fields near the house, but then it hits me. My king was interrogating our prisoners today, and one is more important than the other.

The way Brice tilted his head and his eyes narrowed when I said her name proved as much.

Bring Chiara, Leonardo. Her mate should see her one last time before she stands trial.

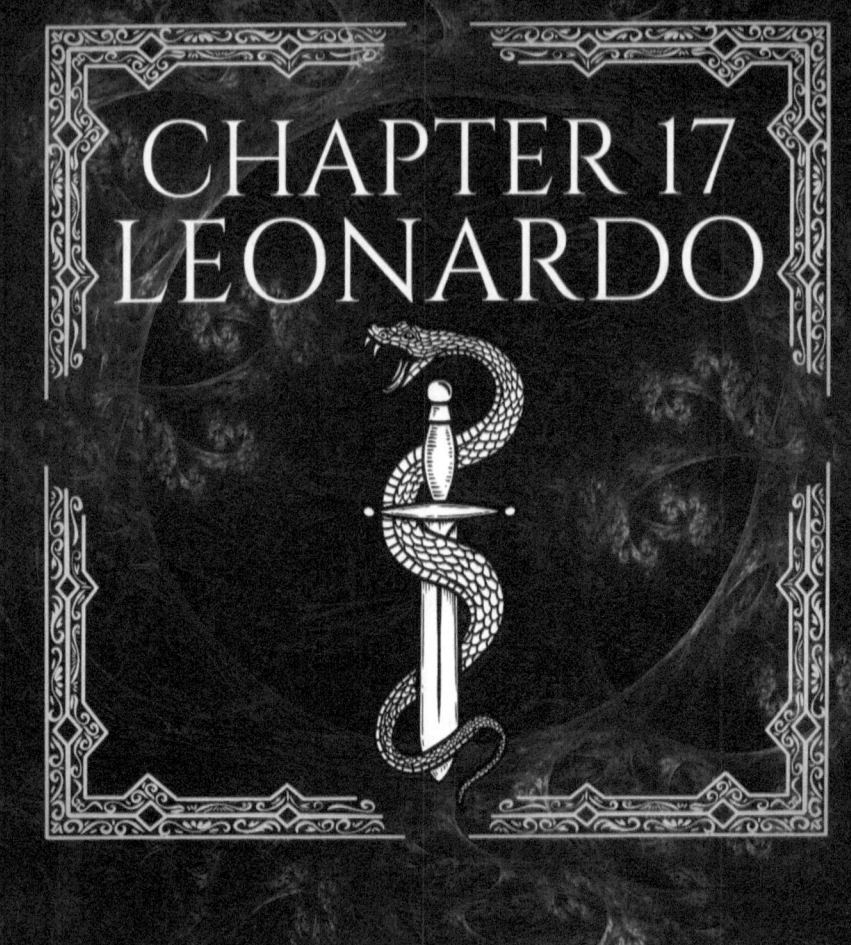

CHAPTER 17
LEONARDO

Going to spend some time with the young ones this
afternoon; I promised them a small foraging expedition
after lessons and a Queen always keeps her promises.
Just like my king. His word is law.
Did I mention I'm still a bit sore? How can I
pencil in a repeat? ;)
It's your turn to play a game of how many licks...

Your precious one.

I chuckle at the sassiness in the Post-It note attached to the mini-refrigerator inside my office. The door to that thing is littered with them; everything from a simple, *Good morning* to *I'll miss you today,* and then my favorite, *Come find me, my king.*

It's possessive and sexy. So sweet and unexpected, but more importantly, something I can't start my day or end my night without again. I'm spoiled by each little note.

Love to walk into a room and find them in random places, then collect each line because, to me, it's a treasure worth showcasing. Just like the happy stickers.

The first time she saw one was a few days after coming to live with me. Isotta's granddaughter had burst into the kitchen showing off her *good behavior* sticker. And my girl, having been deprived of the simplest pleasures, had fallen in love with the goofy things at first sight.

Her smile was radiant. Her excitement was so palpable that I ordered a box filled to the brim with *happy face* stickers that same night, and was excited to go into town the next day and pick up my order from the P.O. box I kept there.

"Leo, what's this?" Her adorable nose scrunches up, her ears twitching in excitement. *"It's very pretty packaging."*

"I think you'll enjoy what's inside the most," I croon, pushing a stray blonde hair back off her cheek. *Her ponytail's a little messy, cheeks flushed with smudges of flour from a baking lesson, and I've never seen anything more beautiful. "Go on. Make your mate happy."*

"You're spoiling me."

"It's my honor to do so, precious one."

"You didn't!" Squeal. Giggling. Tiny hands grip the box with her favorite circular design, and she tucks it against her chest. "Y-you got me stickers?"

"No crying, Anaya," I admonish gently, even as she sniffs happy tears *at me, and then proceeds to place a bright blue monstrosity on her king's forehead, the cartoon winking while blowing a kiss. "I'm never taking this off."*

At that, she snorts. Her grin is so big. "You will, but I'll make sure you start every day for the rest of our days with a smile."

A promise kept. I've never been happier or felt so cared for in my life.

"The prisoners are ready for their interrogation, Your Highness. Ready to go?" Augusto taps the doorframe to my office; *his* excitement is questionable. He's not a blood-thirsty warlock, more diplomatic. "Because I am."

"What's got you so chipper?" I ask, standing from my place behind the desk while tucking today's note into my trouser pocket. "It's not knocking off time yet."

"It's been a while since my Annette executed her role as an elder female." That's all he says before giving me a shrug and then heading back the way he came. He's whistling to himself, too, when I catch up with him and throughout our walk until we reach the dungeons on my territory.

His position as my second-in-command is one he's always taken seriously. Same as his bodyguard duty to protect my mother when she was alive, but this is a side of him that's new. Hilarious, even, but I refrain from calling him out on it and let the man enjoy what he considers foreplay.

A prison employee has the door open for me before I type in the passkey, and it locks behind us just as fast, completely sealing the iron and silver structure housing the last remaining Veltross.

Gabriella and Theodore will arrive tonight, and it will be their choice—their kill—to do with as they please. And while we deal with Chiara and Lena, Xadiel and Isabella are busy cleansing the fae territory of all traces of dark magic. They've made headway inside the royal court with the help of Anaya's grandfather, pushing out those who oppose my mate or fight back against the execution of their prior king, Amelia's father, by the God of War, Ares.

They have no idea the fallen queen is alive yet, and it's just how my beauty wants it. She fears for her mother's life, and Amelia isn't strong enough to defend herself at the moment.

"How painful do you wish the interrogation to be, Leonardo? Annette asked me to procure parameters before you begin."

"At her full discretion." The decision is an easy one to make, at least where this creature is concerned. Because while I'll never condone violence against women, I consider Chiara to be unworthy of any empathy. She helped kill hundreds of innocent, rejected faes. She almost bled Amelia dry and I'm sure was tempted to do the same to my Anaya. *No sympathy from me. None.* "All I ask is that she's alive when Gabby arrives. This is her kill."

"Thank you, sir. I'll relay the message now." He leaves immediately after, while I take my time and walk down to the interrogation room at a leisurely pace. Each of my boot-covered steps is loud on the concrete floor, the thump echoing off the walls announcing my presence. Many take steps back as I pass their cells, and the few that don't are simply frozen in place and don't move an inch to not call attention to themselves.

Yet the sighs of relief that follow almost make me chuckle. Almost, because I watch as Lena and a recuperating Chiara are brought in wearing shackles and no shoes, their clothes filthy. The scent isn't much better, either.

They don't look at me, but the old witch cowers at my glare, nearly toppling her friend over in the urge to get away from me. *Silly old woman.*

"My king," Annette greets me, her hand tweaking a white linen cloth atop a rolling cart. The prisoners watch her, one more nervous than the other. "I'm ready to begin when you—"

The ringing of my phone cuts her off and I shake my head, answering the device and placing it on speaker. There's static coming from the other end, the harsh breathing of someone very angry.

"King Leonardo Moore speaking. How can I help you?"

A laugh filters through the line, familiar—at one point this person was important to me—but now is an enemy. "You have something of mine, Nephew. Taking what doesn't belong to you isn't very nice. I taught you better."

"Took you long enough to call, Marsilla. Why is that?" The thing she birthed tries to yell out for help. Her mouth is all she has as her hands are shackled to bolted hooks on the floor, but Annette stuffs an old hand towel in her mouth, cutting off the inane sound. She tapes it in place, too. "There, much less noise now. What were you saying?"

"Don't make me hurt you, Leonardo. My heart cares for you, child...it doesn't have to be this way." She sounds sincere, but there isn't an iota of *give-a-fucks* where this conniving and horrendous woman is concerned. Silla's taken so much from me, my siblings, and the woman I love. The only thing that will calm the raging thirst for her blood spilled on the ground is her head on a pike; either option works for me. "Return Amelia and Anaya to me, and you can keep my insolent daughter. She can die, the insipid Wiccan babysitter too, but Brice...he is mine. He will be a fine male for me."

A scream rends the air, deep and guttural behind a gag, and I laugh. "You hear that, Chiara? You're nothing more than your mother's pawn. Completely dispensable."

"Do we have a deal, Nephew? Can we call it a truce now?" Impatience bleeds into her tone, an attempt to command me, but I laugh. Loud and deep until tears prick my eyes, and I tap the table once for Annette to begin.

Circling the two women twice, she cocks her head and then walks over to her tray while I place the phone closer; I want the woman I once called my aunt to hear everything. To get angry over my lack of complying.

Lifting the sheet hiding her weapons, Annette picks up a whip and cracks it. The pure-silver claws at the end snap against the bottom of Lena's chair, and the witch pees herself.

"Leonardo! Answer me, child!" Another hard flick of the wrist, and this time, the ends graze the women's ankles. Shallow cuts, nothing a Band-Aid wouldn't fix, but the way they cry out, you'd think I'd cut off a hand. One is muffled, yet loud, while the other begs for mercy.

"Please don't." Lena's shaking and her head is down. "I'll tell you everything. How and who is involved, just don't hurt me."

"And what is everything, Lena? Are you even a Rossi?" To fuck with her, Annette wraps one of the lashes around her neck and tightens, twisting the leather so tight she begins to turn a little purple. "Nod for me if you are." Frantically, Lena does, a hacking cough wracking her chest when she's released, only to watch the same thing happen to Chiara. The Veltross bastard can't do anything but thrash and move, trying to dislodge Annette's hold any way she can, but fails.

One of the cuts my Aya pummeled into Chiara's face splits wide open and then sizzles, the silver tip at the end of the lash digging into her skin. Even those who aren't pure-blooded fae are susceptible to the metal, the poisonous material meant to draw out pain and leave behind ever-lasting scars if it doesn't kill you first.

Moreover, this wretched female won't be alive long enough to show the world her new scars.

"You brought this upon yourself, kid. You hear me, Leo?" Silla's screeching now. So angry for someone who didn't care what happened to her daughter. "I'm going to kill Anaya, your sisters, and every single person who stands in my way. This is my vow, Moore. Pray to the goddess your fae isn't with child when I rip her apart."

"You'll never get close enough to touch her, *Aunt Silla*." Her old title drips with disdain; I'm ashamed of the years she fooled us. Me. How we let Roberto down. "I'm going to enjoy returning the favor. Your daughter is for the murder of my parents. Brice will be for your betrayal and abuse of Uncle Roberto." All movement in the room ceases, the deadly violence in my tone shaking the walls. Causes the floor to crack at the edges. "But you, Marsilla…I'm going to kill you for threatening my sacred mate. That was your biggest mistake. I'll see you soon."

Leonardo, bring patrols and get the children out of the forest. Brice ambushed me, and he's flying us up...

ANAYA

LEONARDO'S ANGRY WITH ME, and it's understandable. He's yelling through our link and running in my direction—he's getting closer—but I cannot allow Alice to be hurt. He'll have to forgive me this one time for defying his need to protect me and our child. I'm sure my *naughty list* will be full once again, but a true queen cares for her people. Sacrifices herself to protect those that can't protect themselves, just as my mother endured years of torture to keep me alive.

Looking down at the children, I try to smile and reassure them that everything will be okay. "I need you to pair up and run back home." Their cherubic faces are fear-stricken, a few whimpering. "No stopping. No looking back. And if you see guards along the way, tell them what happened."

I get multiple nods as my wings unfurl, catching the rays of sunshine. Prisms appear in various places, the little seedlings popping from the ground in a line of tiny green leaves, and for that brief second, they smile. *They're going to be okay, Anaya. Go!*

"Go, little ones. I'll see you soon."

"Please bring her back," one boy whispers, and the others follow, getting riled up when I need them to remain calm. To listen. "Please, Queen Anaya. My cousin is small and—"

"Kiddos, I will never allow any of you to be hurt." Kneeling at their level, I make sure to look them each in the eyes. "Trust me, and do as I say. Now run home so I can fly up and find her."

At once they rush to hug me, surrounding me with their pure love before taking heed and running as fast as their tiny legs can carry them. Once they're past the tree line, my wings stretch and shake themselves out—I take off. The wind feels good across my skin, a part of me I miss, but this isn't a flight meant for joy and I'm hot on Brice's tail before he can get close to the coast.

Being smaller, I'm faster than him. It takes no time to eat up the space between us; I've always had an agility that few can match when in flight. Flying is like dancing to me, a rhythm and pulse that lives and breathes inside my veins, and in seconds, he's within my reach.

I don't hesitate to land on his back, throwing his balance off, the damage to his wings at the hands of my mate making it uneasy for him to keep stability. Our fall is fast, yet Alice keeps her eyes on me while I wink, making sure she knows I'm here.

"I've got you," I mouth, and she gives me a half-wink type of response that's silly and adorable at the same time. Both eyes really just blink at me with a side tilt of her head, but that's enough for me to concentrate on the irate general. I also ask her to cover her ears by placing my palms over mine, knowing he'll try to get at me with insults before attacking.

"Get the fuck off, Anaya." Meaty paws swipe at me and miss, but I reward the effort by digging my knee harder into the injured left wing, then the right so they're even while thanking the Gods I had the foresight to communicate with her. "This is not the way to win my forgiveness, and I'm going to fuck you raw and make you bleed for this disobedience. I don't need you ruining what—"

"Watch your mouth, Brice."

"Ma princesse, you're pushing it."

"And you bore me with the same rhetoric. Why are you here?"

"We're going home. Your rightful place is—"

"What about your mate?" For a second he freezes, dropping a few dozen feet in altitude, but regains his composure. He doesn't say anything after, but I notice he's edging closer to a rocky area that if we crash into would be fatal for Alice.

I need to get her out of here.

Leonardo, I'm going to circle back, and he's going to be pissed. Be ready.

I'm lucky the brute doesn't have enough sense to secure the one thing I'm endangering my life to save. He tossed the child over his shoulder like a small sack of carrots, her body barely held by his hand on her ankle, and I capitalize on the idiocy when I *oh so gently* stab his eye with my blunt fingernail.

Ready, Aya. And baby, I love you so much for saving one of our young, and I'm going to show you just how proud I am when I turn your ass red.

"You fucking cunt!" Brice snarls, but releases her immediately and Alice catches air, rising high enough that I snatch her up and push off his mangled brown wings, turning my body at the last second to head back in the direction we came. Clouds graze our sides while she tucks her small face into my neck, hiding from the man hurtling threats at me.

"Ma princesse, I tire of these games. You need to come with me and take your place at my feet."

"No." *How many indiscretions are you adding?*

His chuckle is all I get as a response, and it sends a shiver down my spine, one that causes me to let up on my speed and for Brice's fingers to grip the tip of my wing.

That's his second mistake of the day because he's falling at a rapid speed a second later when lightning strikes.

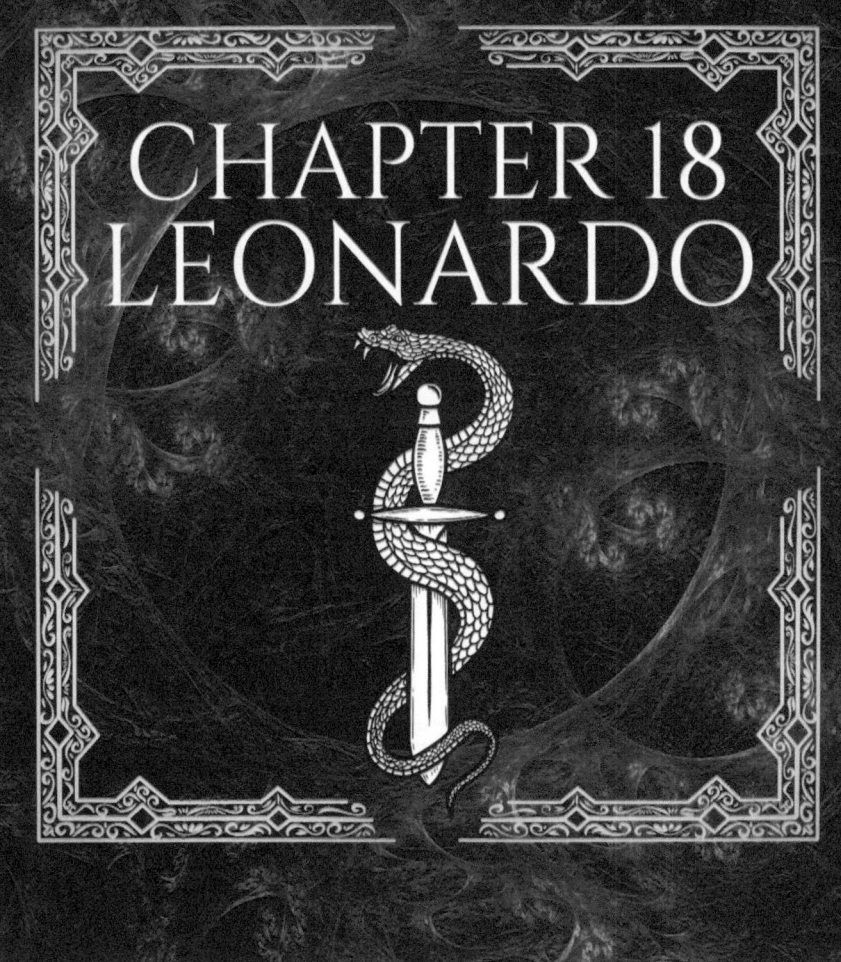

CHAPTER 18
LEONARDO

I've never been so angry and scared in my life than when I caught sight of Anaya taking flight after that son of a bitch. I'd been seconds from keeping her grounded. We'll bring him down another way, but my female shows once again how truly worthy of adoration she is.

She didn't think twice about rescuing one of the smallest members of our coven. The same little girl who laughs with Aya over stickers and cookies and *oohs* over pretty flowers, as Alice calls them.

That little witchling gives my mate hope. Helps her see what a healthy and happy childhood can be, something my queen is passionate about. Something she speaks often about when it's just the two of us inside our bedroom with the lights off at night. She speaks freely and from the heart, a private confession that breaks my heart yet fills me with so much tender love for her.

"There's nothing more precious than watching them discover who they are without the prejudice of the world knocking them down. To let them explore and get messy and know that no matter what they do, there will be no disappointment, but rather affectionate correction. There's no need to terrorize a child into doing what you want them to, because when you accept who they are, what you get is more than you ever hoped for. I never want to see another clipped wing in my life, Leonardo. I want our children and those of our people to be truly free."

That doesn't mean we won't be having an insightful and hands-on discussion about this afterward, but for now, I keep track of her movements. She's dropping faster than I'm happy with, little Alice tucked in against her chest while the idiot beneath my boot lies still.

He passed out before crashing, an effect of the lightning strike, and this new power is still a bit volatile. It feeds heavily on my emotions. Gives the sensation of a thousand snakes wrapping around every inch of your body, their bodies burning hot before striking out on the object of my ire.

Brice is exuding a bit of smoke while his clothes are singed, and I take great joy in giving him a second strike while Chiara watches. How she whimpers when his damaged wings, one side destroyed, crack under the pressure of my foot. She's on her knees mere feet from us, so much pain in her traitorous, tear-brimmed eyes, but the vampiric side of her doesn't allow them to fall.

Instead, they gather and gather.

"Does it hurt to see him like this?" I ask her, but she doesn't respond. She's frozen. Yet when my female lands a few seconds later, her body in my outstretched arms with a smiling Alice giggling, I see the first sign of fire in Chiara since bringing her out to witness the idiot's demise.

Chiara screams and tries to rush to her feet, clumsily fumbling closer, and no one moves to stop her. The guards around us chuckle a bit. The once put-together and snobby woman doesn't raise empathy from anyone, much less their queen.

Anaya looks at her with annoyance and hands the small child over to Isotta, who's been on pins and needles with worry. My precious one understands this and gives the older witch a touch of the hand, much like I do to those in my aegis, and everyone gasps.

There's so much joy and pride coming from those present. So much to celebrate as the wind sweeps past us, carrying a hint of patchouli and lavender—my parents—and they too, are grateful for her. She's what we've been missing all these years.

Soon, we'll have our binding ceremony and put all of this behind us.

"Please take the child and stay indoors, Isotta. Take two guards and after they drop you off back home, they'll stay outside your home."

"Thank you, my queen."

"Mmph!" The tribrid's muffled scream is pitiful at best, but has to hurt and she grimaces, wanting to reach for her neck but can't. The shackles she wears are laced with iron and silver, painful to her, and the most minute shift is burning her flesh. A lesson she's learned the hard way, having fallen on her ass this time beside the piece-of-merde male she loves.

No bite mark, though…

Tapping my arm, Anaya wiggles to be put down. "Just for a second. I know I'm in trouble."

"Oh, you most definitely are, but—" A portal opens about twenty feet from us, and Tero slips through. In his mouth, there's a flag. It's solid black; I can scent traces of Gabriella and Isabella on it, but more important is what it stands for.

Mors.

Death.

––––––––

THE FAE REALM is in utter chaos when we arrive. The screams and the sound of fighting can be heard for miles while the knocked-out bodies of Brice and Chiara are dumped together in the middle of the throne room. The elders hiss at the sight then shut their mouths just as quickly. These sympathizers of Larue's doctrine who'd taken over the castle are shocked when Amelia, head held high, walks in after me beside Anaya and her father.

The true fae monarchs don't look at anyone. They continue the path past the elders who've spent their time cursing Anaya and her mother, the very woman who nearly lost her life at the hands of the man they idolize.

Past the gilded thrones and to the left, there's an open balcony where the cacophony of protesters are crying out in anger. These are the people who've been hurt the most; the lower-ranking and small shop owners who have paid the steepest price during Larue's reign.

They have been used and at times abused by a male-driven authoritarian regime that doesn't care about anything but power and how to create a false narrative of riches that don't exist. Because saying something is true doesn't necessarily make it so, and this is one kingdom that's suffered over a stack of lies that's shattered without repair.

"Watch the balcony, my king."

"As you wish, my heart." Lifting her hand, I press a kiss to each knuckle before offering Anaya my arm. Her grandfather is helping Amelia; their relationship isn't healed yet, but at the very least the former queen has been speaking to him via phone calls. And like her daughter, the device has been a joyous novelty for her. She has become obsessed with emojis and has no shame in adding fifteen per message.

Her grandfather isn't innocent in that department either. With each new thing he learns or discovers, the disappointment grows. Eats him slowly. Their kingdom hasn't progressed much in the last hundred and twenty years, stuck living in a time that the rest of the world has left behind.

These people don't know about the internet or mobile phones, much less computers.

And while the family has touched on the subject in the past, it's Anaya who pushes the agenda.

"The newer generations deserve the opportunity to grow past the walls of our kingdom. They should have the right to the same level of education and opportunities as other creatures. To do so, we need to expand. Bring technology in and move toward a new beginning where equality is key, and no one is looked down upon because of what they have between their legs."

"Thank you." **Bend down and give me your cheek, Leonardo.**

With a hand bent in front of my waist and one bent behind my back, I bow for her and I'm rewarded with kisses. One to my cheek. One to my chin. One to the tip of my nose. Moreover, the men do not like it, if the looks they give us are anything to go by, but they don't do anything else.

These fae males aren't fighters or warriors, and I don't believe they've ever held a weapon in their lives. I am, however, biding my time. Just waiting for the minimalist excuse to knock their pompous asses out.

These assholes forgot what it is to be a real man.

A text pings as Anaya steps out with her family onto the balcony. They are standing side by side—a united front—and silence ensues. The protestors calm, and I pull out my cell phone and read Isabella's message.

> The castle is surrounded; Xadiel and Theo are not
> far. They've taken out a small cluster of anti-Anaya
> troublemakers near the southern border and are
> making their way back. ~Isa

Three dots appear as I begin to type. It starts and stops three times before her second message arrives.

> They have the bodies with them as proof. Not one
> of them is fae. Two vampires and three witches,
> the latter having the Rossi insignia on their cloaks.
> ~Isa

> Don't bother responding. Keep your eyes on the
> man with the bronze lion's head pin on his lapel.
> He's not to be trusted. ~Isa

I find the asshole in question sitting directly in the middle of the courtiers' section, a designated section containing three rows of seating for males of an upper rank. No faction representative is here, and there are no visitors or special guests—just them. They'd planned a coup while Anaya risked her left to save Alice, and putting two and two together isn't leaving an understanding warlock in their midst.

He was a diversion while Silla used these aristocratic suckers as the means to finally take control of the throne. They did all the work, and Marsilla hoarded the reward. *But where is she hiding?*

It's not far, though. To her detriment, the years spent taking care of me created a bond—a tie—that allows me to sense when she's within a certain distance of me. It happens with my brothers-in-law and those closest to me, like Augusto—it's nothing like what I share with my sisters and much less than with my Anaya—I know she's within this building.

Signaling with my hand, I hold up three fingers and my guards spread out to protect every possible entryway. Some are carrying swords, while others choose to use nothing but magic or hand-to-hand combat.

A low murmur catches my attention, and it grows the longer my girl and her family are out on that balcony, the chant of *Amelia* and *Anaya* rising in volume and shaking the ground we're standing on. Their people are clamoring for help. To right the wrongs committed, but they have no idea that changes have already been implemented.

The city has been cleansed of black magic, and there are daily sweeps to keep it that way.

The kingdom has new laws coming into effect by the dawn of day tomorrow.

All the men seated inside this room will cease to breathe unless they bend their knees.

Amidst the screaming and jubilation, my mate walks back in and takes the head seat.

Not her grandfather or her mother, but her. It's being done this way on purpose—this moment had already been in talks between the trio, but Anaya wanted her mother to be stronger before she walks these halls again. Not that it matters now; all these opportunistic worms did was anger my heart, and the time to end this has come.

Long live my queen.

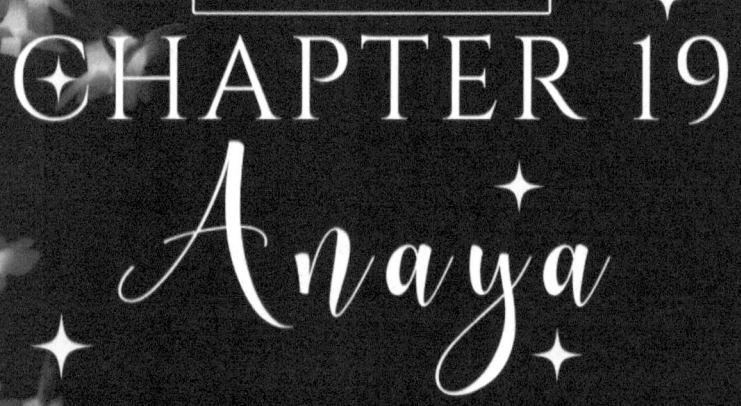

CHAPTER 19

Anaya

They're on their way, precious one. Just a few minutes.

Looking out across the room, I'm saddened by the lack of representation in attendance.

All men. All with money.

Not a single representative from a faction or a business owner—anyone other than this lot.

These men have lived the high life while others suffer. Males who do not care about the concerns or needs of their brethren because keeping the status quo is more important. Lining their pockets on the blood, sweat, and tears of those who do not have a voice, or if they do, it's a limited one.

It's disgusting. It's something I grew up dealing with and internally fighting against—to not wake up one day and think this is *acceptable*. The norm.

"No more." All eyes turn to me, waiting to see if I'll say anything else, but I just look at them. At those who came here today to try and steal my maman's throne—my birthright—to hand it over to the only woman they respect. *Why her?*

I've asked myself that question many times over the years.

Why does *she* have a seat at the table?

Why do they follow her word as if it were Larue's?

What is she offering in exchange for this kind of loyalty?

"Princesse, what is going on here?" A man stands from his seat, his head held high and back straight. His eyes sweep the room, and when he reaches Leonardo, his top lip curls in abhorrence. "Why have you stormed our sacred grounds with this filth? Your father—"

"Speak when spoken to, Jean." His face turns red, eyes narrowing on me, but backs down when my mate takes his place behind my chair. Another sign of his respect and loyalty to me. "Now sit. Not another word until my guests arrive."

"What guests! This is a—" Lightning strikes a large portrait of Larue, lighting it on fire. It cuts off the protest of another man. I've never seen him before, but I do catch an amulet tucked beneath his dress shirt. Like the others worn by the elders, it's become dull in the days since the blood bank closed.

He's also younger, maybe my age, and I'm wondering who brought him in.

I watch him while the picture burns bright, and I have no doubt in my mind that Leo is manipulating the contained flames—a theory proven a minute later when I swear a happy face appears within the fire.

Is that you? In response, I get a hand on my shoulder and an opal dagger placed on my lap. Another insult to these men; a woman with a weapon.

Beside me, Maman recognizes the piece and gasps; I'd forgotten to mention it being in our possession and how it came to be, but there's time for that later as more portraits are damaged and the royal blue double doors are thrown open, revealing a bloody vampire and werewolf carrying the dead bodies of four men and one woman.

And just like we did with Brice and Chiara, my brothers-in-law dump the bodies where they're visible to *all*. The action wakes up Veltross's daughter—the woman screams at the sight of bloody bodies so close to her, one man's arm touching her leg.

"Oh my God!" she screeches at the top of her lungs, dragging herself back as best she can, only to bump into the dead woman. That makes her stop. This death affects her. "No. No!"

"Fuck, shut up," Brice snarls, groaning awake and trying to sit up, but the pain makes him hiss. His fall left him battered and bruised while the lightning burned certain areas of his skin. "What the hell happened?"

"I'm glad you could join us." Their heads simultaneously turn in my direction and then flick throughout the room. They take in my family and their accomplices before coming back to me:

A tiny fae with no knowledge of how to run this trial and who's dressed in a pair of ripped-at-the-knee denim overalls, a white crop top, and on my feet, some Chuck Taylor's in the color pink.

My hair is in a French braid and I have on the mascara and gloss I put on before leaving the coven house to meet with the witchlings. Our excursion demanded comfort and after ruining the clothes I flew in, I changed into this. Just as cute and perfect for kicking ass and taking names, as I learned on social media.

The things I've learned over the last few months are mind-blowing. Changed me.

"Ma princesse, you are making a fool of yourself. End this now." A demand—hissing at me—something my mate doesn't approve of, and he jumps over my throne and rushes him, plowing his knee into Brice's face.

"Son of a bitch," Brice bellows, the pain-filled groan causing *his* mate to whimper, a sound I don't think she was supposed to make.

For some reason, they didn't want anyone to know of their relationship. *Why?*

"Disrespect her again, asshole. I dare you." Leonardo's voice is lethal, his body poised to knee him again as he grips the injured man's hair and forces his head back. Looks him in the eye. "Go on. Say something."

"Don't hurt him!" Chiara tries to crawl over a body but gags and falls back, crying her frustration. "Let him go!"

"Who is he to you, Chiara? Why do you care?" She doesn't answer me, swallowing hard and looking away. *Why won't you admit it?* "Is that the game you want to play? Will you deny your mate?"

I give her a full five minutes but she doesn't respond, and I lift my hand high in the air. That signals Gabriella and Isabella's entrance, a demure Lena two steps behind them.

The older witch looks haggard—exhaustion seeps from her every pore—and I motion for her to take a seat in an empty chair in the courtiers' section.

At once they stand and complain, giving Lena dirty looks while flashing their fangs, but they quickly fall into line when six creatures growl so loud the floor shakes.

Theodore and Xadiel thump their chests and crouch, ready to snap the first neck of many tonight, while Leonardo's beast is just as volatile. Storms rage outside, lightning crackling too close for comfort, and Chiara whimpers again.

The men do so as well.

"Lena, please take a seat. I have some questions I want answers for."

"Yes, Queen Anaya." Warily, Lena sits and exhales slowly, trying to calm herself. "I'm ready."

"Good." Giving Leo a nod, he brings Brice to my feet and forces his head down to the floor. Pins him there. "How did Chiara end up with the Rossi coven? For what purpose?"

"Marsilla wanted to keep her close without actually bonding with the Miss. She didn't trust the vampires not to scent her true bloodline and kill her before her purpose was fulfilled."

"What purpose?"

"To marry Leonardo." I'm not surprised in the least by Lena's answer. The way she behaved when we met—the looks sent his way…Chiara believes him hers.

"Shut up! Not another…mhhp!"

Gabriella's covering her mouth while lifting her off the floor by the grip on her face. Her usually green eyes are blood red, and her fangs are bared. "Quiet."

"Continue, Lena."

Tears roll down the woman's face, chin trembling. "I'm so sorry."

"No. You're not, but that's not what I asked of you." I lean forward while pointing at Chiara Veltross. "What was her full purpose? What happened after she *mated* with King Moore? What about her mate?"

"They couldn't be together in public, so they'd cheat on their chosen, same as Larue did to your mother. Biting wouldn't be allowed, but they'd still have sex as often as the bond demanded it. At least, until one of you died." Again, growls and snarls reverberated throughout the room. She cowers, almost toppling over, but manages to stay upright. "It's hard to explain with them—"

"I'm going to stop you right there. You're not here to help anyone, but to answer my questions in exchange for a life in a secluded cabin with no outside communication until the day you cease to exist. That was the deal: total honesty, and I'll allow you to continue breathing."

"Yes, Queen Anaya."

"I will not correct you again. Tell me everything, or I'll let Theodore rip your throat out. I've promised him more than one prey today, and I plan to deliver."

"Please don't kill me." Pitiful, yet I won't deny her distress tugs at my heart. I'm not a cold person, it's just not who I am, but I also can't put those I love at risk. "It started before Gabriella and King Astor met. Veltross made comments of wanting to overthrow the vampire ruler, and word got back to King Larue. They met a few times, made plans, and brought together greedy coven leaders—my family being one of them. Moreover, it didn't take long for them to be tempted by the golden trap swinging right in front of their eyes." Pausing, she squeezes her fingers together. Digs them into her lap. "For them to kill our former king and priestess."

"Where were you during that time?"

"Here." At my perplexed expression, she continues. "I was kept in a room on Larue's wing while the attacks occurred. The backup plan needed to be secured, that's why we integrated ourselves after the fact. Because we truly were out of the country."

"Are there any more members of the Veltross family alive?" Her eyes shift to the woman on the ground. "Not anymore."

"Who was she?"

"A cousin." She didn't elaborate, but Chiara screamed as Gabriella pried open her lips and ripped out a piece of her tongue, helping to jog the old woman's memory with the use of fear. "She's a second cousin. Her name is Bianca, and she was overeager, from the times we spoke to her. Bianca didn't believe in the intermingling of the species and hated her queen. Was a little jealous of her, even though her mate, Giulio, was a good guard. She contacted Silla to help."

"Did she not know Chiara's a tribrid?" An explosion of anger comes from Brice, and I click my tongue; I don't like being interrupted. He's cursing, trying to buck my mate off, and I just want to be done with them all. To never see this abhorrent bunch again, and for once in my life, I take a page out of my father's playbook.

Rising, I grip the legacy opal dagger on my lap and walk down to my mate. He's watching me with an arched brow but doesn't ask me any questions. "Lift his head."

"As you wish, precious one." Grip firm on Brice's head, he

extends his neck back, exposing it to me. Puts his in a position to meet my stare. "Is that good enough?"

"Yes." The blade glints in the room's lighting, and the blue tones within the opal are vibrant as I cut my palm and then swipe the sharp metal across the sanguine drop. I'm feeding the blade so it recognizes its owner, but also to make this just a little more insulting.

They've wanted our blood for their sick purpose, but now he can wear it for the rest of his life. Not that he has long; Brice must die.

He's a threat to my family. To my mate and baby.

And because my child likes to make an entrance, they chose that moment to let their presence be known. They've done this a few times, quiet themselves all day—when we're around others—but the moment we're alone, his or her heart beats strongly.

A *thump, thump, thump* that never fails to bring a smile to my face. Like now, amidst this chaos, here's my beautiful little one showing me the way.

"You're pregnant? You fucking cu—" Brice is cut off mid-insult by the tip of my blade slicing through his skin from chin to tongue, and I leave it at that. There will be no greater *insult* to him than being silenced by me. "I am with child, yes. But that's not what's important. Tell me, did Larue know you weren't of pure fae blood?" Hushed whispers start in the courtiers' section, words of outrage at my audacity, but none of them stand up or demand I stop. Their fear doesn't allow it. "The blade seared your flesh, Brice. Your blood isn't tinted blue like mine and that of every fae here. So I wonder… what are you? Maybe half-human."

Not a question. This misogynistic purist is a liar, and the proof is in his blood. The scent, thickness, and color all point to him having human traits.

"Silla, please! Stop this!" A little garbled from the missing chunk of tongue, but her words were clear. Words I agree with. *Yes, please. Show your face.* "You promised we wouldn't be hurt. You swore you'd protect me."

"Goddess, you don't get it yet, do you?" Lena deadpans, body visibly shuddering. "Even when Silla was pregnant, you were accepted as nothing more than a spare. All parties knew it'd be useful to have a fall-back plan *just in case*, but Elise was always the first choice." At the mention of the older Veltross daughter, Gabriella takes what's left of Chiara's tongue and tosses it at Brice's head. It lands on the top and then slides down his temple, leaving another bloody mark behind. "She was to seduce King Astor, but Chiara would be for Leonardo. Marsilla has always been adamant about that union. She cares for King Moore."

CHAPTER 20
LEONARDO

End him.

Anaya's voice filters in my head, and it's the sweetest demand. I've been holding back for her sake, keeping the bloodlust—the desire to cleanse this room with his life's essence—at bay, but no more. The opal dagger embedded a few inches deep, not enough to kill, slides a little deeper when I lower his head down to the ground again.

This asshole will never have the pleasure of seeing my beautiful mate again.

He doesn't deserve any dignity.

Yet before the blade passes an inch past the roof of his mouth, I remove it altogether and smash his face into the marble floors. There's a sickening crunch that follows, more blood smearing the once-clean floors. "You can confirm before I slit your throat. Are you half-human?"

The bang of the doors being shoved open calls everyone's attention to the entrance, but I saw his nod and so did Aya. Silla's standing there, and she isn't alone. General Francois is behind her and nudges the woman I once considered family forward. She's lost a bit of weight since the last time I saw her, but the smile reserved for me since I was young is ever-present.

"Put the knife down, Leonardo. This isn't you, piccolo."

"Walk, Marsilla." He shoves her forward, and she stumbles a bit but is held upright by Uncle Roberto who rushes to her aid. He straightens her, and it's heartbreaking to see him fuss over the same woman who spent years torturing him. Roberto's looking her over to see if she's injured while emitting unintelligible noises that show his distress.

I'm confused by it. We all are.

"Please stand back, sir." Francois makes to gently push him aside, but my uncle will have none of it, and Anaya waves him off from her throne. The general heeds her simple request without an issue and takes a protective stance to the right of the dais where her family sits.

Her mother and grandfather haven't said a word, but their expressions speak volumes. They're embarrassed by the very people their family has devoted their lives to serving, and that has to be a painful reality to swallow. More so for the old man who helped destroy what he's built in his time as ruler.

I've seen the guilt in his eyes, and it runs just as deep today as it did the day he woke up in the hospital room. He's reminded every time he looks at his daughter. When he hears Anaya speak.

And now, as so many of the elders here wear the same amulet without knowing the truth.

They've been manipulated. Lied to. Stolen from.

"You've desecrated our ancient laws, Anaya. This little show has proven that you're not fit to lead." Jean stands amid the bunch, eyes bouncing from her to me. "We request you step down and leave our lands at once."

"You don't have the right to so much as request a glass of water in my kingdom."

"Your father—"

"Is dead. His son is dead." She tilts her head, appraising him. "You'll be dead soon, too."

"How dare you!" Others rise, too. A united front. "Look at the bodies and the blood…you've killed our innocent people in the ill-intended quest to destroy us."

"Those brought in by King Xadiel and King Astor are *not* fae. Let's not play games here."

"How would you know, unless you planted these imposters?"

"Or maybe you've all forgotten how to use common sense." Her sass rubs them wrong; I'm sure they've never encountered a mouthy Anaya before. It's a huge change from the scared and bruised woman I met a few short months ago. Now, my precious one is confident, funny, and happy. My queen thrives. "They have no pointy ears, they bleed red and black, they do not carry the lingering undertone of honey in their scents. That scent marker is only detectable to us."

"Then what are they? Why are they here?"

"You tell me why I have vampires and witches running rampant through my kingdom, executing random acts of violence, and one just so happens to be a Veltross?"

"I don't—"

"Shut up." Her voice carries the weight of a command, and I smile as he's forced to do as she asks. "I don't want to hear another lie or attempt to discredit me when, quite frankly, you're wasting your breath. No one here cares. I don't, and neither does my family."

Give the signal, Anaya. It's time.

With a gentle hold of her hand, Roberto walks Silla over to me.

They stand to my left while I hold the blade at Brice's throat, lazily sliding in and out of the wound my precious one created.

Something I'm so proud of her for doing. For defending *herself* and not just everyone she loves.

"Now, Brothers." The moment those two words slip past Aya's mouth, Theo and Xadiel rush the elders, their bodies nothing but a blur. Their claws are out, and a blueish mist permeates the air as shallow cuts are made across the necks and chests of the men wearing the amulet.

Each stone is tossed to the ground and crushed beneath the heavy weight of an angry beast's footstep. And as soon as they crack and splinter, the men who'd worn the chains crumble to the ground. More than two-thirds of the elders drop in mere seconds, and all to the background chorus of the cries coming from the open balcony: *long live the queen.*

Cornered and afraid, those that remain run toward the exits, but the guards stop them—some with magic, and others with the threat of meeting the sharp end of a blade, forcing those smart enough to comprehend the severity to drop to their knees.

All but one man. He refuses to submit.

Keep your eyes on the man with the bronze lion's head pin on his lapel. He's not to be trusted.

Instead of trying to escape, Jean thought the distraction would help him reach Anaya. In his single-minded quest, he removed the bronze lapel pin and raised it high above his head, ready to drill into hers with its long-neck design—three inches of metal with a sharpened point so it slips through fabric easily without damaging the piece. It's meant to hang in place, but now he's aiming for her face, and I'm thankful for Xadiel who reaches them first. He's there before I can throw myself at or fry the soon-to-be-dead male.

A furred arm with black-tipped claws punches a hole through Jean's spine, ripping out his heart while Anaya's grandfather steps between them. The point of the pin stabs the old king's back, but he simply shakes it off while cupping Aya's face and asking if she's *okay*.

It's over in seconds.

Amelia doesn't move, though. She's stuck frozen, and it's just too soon for her to be back here.

Jean never had time to scream, but Silla does. In anger. Outrage.

She's watching everything she connived for fall, and it's permanent disgrace.

We're not done.

Brice bleeds out slowly as the knife wound creates a puddle beneath his head. It's a solitary ending for him. We haven't allowed him to see her—his mate—who's been unable to do anything but whimper since losing her tongue. Said appendage lies a mere inch from us.

"It wasn't supposed to be like this," he murmurs, coughing a bit. "Larue should've drowned them. Slit your mate's throat and bled her dry, bathed in her blood before tossing her in the lake."

"That's a great idea. Slicing of a throat," I whisper menacingly and turn him to face the room with two purposes in mind: sparing Anaya from seeing what I'm about to do, and so the fated pair can watch the other die. "Is this better?"

"Fuck you, witch!"

I drag the tip of the blade two inches lower and slice through from one end to the other. Slowly. Peeling through layers, and when I feel the change from flesh to the more solid mass of the trachea, I slip my fingers inside. I stretch and prod as he cries out, thrashing from his face-down position on the floor.

"Leonardo, stop this. Call off your bitch." Another death comes then, and it's her daughter this time, ripped apart—right down the middle—by the first couple they sought to ruin. Gabriella and Theodore each hold up half a body in their hands. The head stayed with Theodore, though.

Why? No clue, but I finally see the cracking of Silla's façade. *This hurt her.*

Maybe not because of love, but because she's alone. No lackeys to do her dirty work.

Isabella looks between the bodies and Xadiel moves them into a pile, one head standing out among the dead. *Giulio.* But where the others are struck with an expression of terror, he looks at peace. Resigned.

Once Chiara's remains are tossed at the top, my sister lights the pyre. One I help burn bright when lighting strikes a growing spark, creating a mini explosion of blue.

The hottest flame.

The scent of burnt flesh permeates the air while I yank out Brice's throat. I toss it at Silla's feet, delighting in the way she screeches and jumps back into Roberto's chest, clinging to his arm.

"Roberto, get me out of here," she cries out, stepping back as Anaya leaves her seat and walks up to me. We're almost the same height this way, my body kneeling while she stands tall and regal. Her small, delicate hand cups my cheek, and this time, she bends the tiniest fraction to kiss my lips. One small peck.

Toss him in.

What's left of Brice is mangled, charred, and disgusting—just as he was in real life.

He's not worth the effort to burn, but I toss him in just the same as a semi-circle forms around Marsilla. Our entire family stands and looks at her, letting her see that she didn't win.

"Roberto, do something. Please!" His nod is barely perceptible, and Silla breathes out a sigh of relief when he spreads a hand out to push us back. I want to intercept, to snap him out of whatever bullshit she's got him under, when Isabella whispers *don't*.

My eyes snap to hers, and she's smiling. Devilishly so.

Whatever she's seen is just and we'll abide by it, even if I'd love nothing more than to grant Anaya and Amelia their rightful kill. The latter of which joins us, and for the first time since arriving here, she smiles.

"I'm okay, ma cherie. Today is a day of celebration." Tears brim her eyes; you can feel her pain over all the lives lost, but there's peace in all that hurt. "No more. It ends here."

"Roberto, let go of my arm. You're hurting me, my love!" Silla's fighting Roberto who has a firm grip on her left forearm, pulling her closer to the fire. He's trying to soothe her as best he can, stroking his thumb in small sweeps, but she's unappreciative of the act. Instead, Marsilla thrashes and smacks his arm and then uses her fist, pummeling his side.

My uncle is relentless as he marches them toward the flame, close enough to feel the roaring heat when he cups her face. He stares at her with a soft grin before mouthing, *I loathe you.*

"Roberto, what do you mean? You're my…no!" Coldly, he tosses her in along with Larue's followers and her kin. Agonized screams rend the air; she's fighting to get out, but he holds her in place, not caring about injuring himself or dying. Doesn't so much as flinch at her desperate cries or the fake promise of a future life together. And I want to stop it, pull him back, but a hand grips the back of my shirt and I look back from over my shoulder.

"He will live. I swear it, and what a happy life it will be."

Through curses and cries and large burns on his arms, he keeps her in place until her last breath. And even then, Roberto waits a few more seconds to make sure. Only then does he pull back and collapse on the floor as a group of fae storm the room and simultaneously, the fire goes out.

Who turned it off, I have no clue, but a woman wearing a chef's jacket rushes in with a wooden rolling pin held high, her helpers a few steps from her. They survey the scene in horrific awe. Those who dropped to their knees are being led out by Francois, but it's the unconscious warlock in her sights.

"Mate."

He's being given a second chance.

EPILOGUE #1

Anaya

Sometimes the best things in life are unexpected.

A surprise visit from a loved one.

A warm hug just because.

Or maybe it's meeting the man of my dreams at a time when I had nothing left to give.

It's the sweetest gift. The true meaning of the word blessing. And it's because of him that I've found my true purpose in life, the meaning of where I begin and now end—a prosperous life where all paths lead to this wonderful man that I'm proud to call mine.

My love. An amazing father. My king.

I cherish and vow to protect his heart as he does mine. I give freely and ask for nothing because true love has no boundaries, just honest devotion.

That's how I feel about my Leonardo.

He's everything to me. To our family.

"He's so precious, Aya. The kid is going to steal the show at your ceremony," Gabriella coos at her nephew, tickling his little toes as I slip his baby tuxedo pants over his diapered butt and then adjust the matching sash. The little man will be wearing a replica of his father's outfit, down to the embroidered cloak with a hood and a bare chest underneath. "As his queen, who do you think will wear it better?"

"My son. Hands down." It's not even a contest. My son is going to steal the show at his parents' binding ceremony. "I cannot wait to have them take a selfie."

This original and his mini duo are my life.

Tanix Paolo Moore was born five months ago, kicking and screaming, and was without a doubt the cutest baby grump. His wrinkly face brought so much to our lands; both Fae and Wiccan rejoiced equally with the arrival of our new prince.

His aunts and uncles spoil him, too, just as we adore our niece and nephew, mini dictators that they are, like their fathers. Toddlers don't mess around; I've seen and heard things, and I pray my Tanix will have mercy on my soul because the men in our family are the *good cops* in every scenario.

"They grow up too fast." Isa holds out a finger for mon petit prince to grab and he does, wiggling around and giggling as three women fuss and *ahh* over every little thing he does. "But we'll have more kids soon. All of us, in fact, so plenty of years to adore the little monarchs."

"How soon, Isa?" Gabby asks before scooping up her daughter and kissing her soft cheeks. Beloved giggles at that, tiny fangs peaking through baby gums and she's barely two. "Like I should be watching out for…?"

Her sister snorts and shrugs. "You'll know. Chasing leads to pregnancy."

"I'm not even going to ask." For the fae, the full term of a pregnancy is longer than for other species. Our offspring need their mothers until the tenth month, and childbirth is always done naturally. No magic. No pain medication. It's a ritual that's carried over for generations and one of the few in the newly formed council, elected by the people, refuses to change at the behest of mothers.

The pain is intense, but worth it and it's a badge of honor to all fae women.

Another change is the right to marry for love. No more bartering or political arrangements; matings will occur for bonded pairs unless a mate is chosen, not fated, and both parties are in love.

They don't happen often, but love is love, and I want my people to have a choice. That if you're abused, or have been wronged, a dissolution of a union is also available to all.

They have upgraded electrical grids for all, not just my family's castle. They have internet and phones and access to a wealth of knowledge they never knew existed.

But more than that, both kingdoms—Wiccan and Fae—can travel between countries and packs or covens without the fear of persecution or prejudice. All are welcome. All are protected under a peace treaty signed by the rulers of the wolves, vampires, fae, and witches.

"You'll know, but you can blame it on a little too much wine one night." Rolling my eyes at her suggestively knowing look, I step back and head toward the master bathroom where my dress for the ceremony hangs behind the door.

No one has seen it.

I chose the satin floor-length slip dress after an outing to the werewolf kingdom. We'd walked into Isa's favorite boutique, a she-wolf-owned store that I fell in love with immediately. It was open and warm, and every article of clothing was simply exquisite with its chosen textiles and patterns, the flattering shapes that complimented a woman's body.

I've never wanted to buy everything in sight before, but I was very close to spending a small fortune that day. My first real shopping spree. I perused the racks for hours that day, looking for something to wear to Isabella and Xadiel's re-do ceremony, as she calls it, when I found it.

My dress. The one I'd wear on the night of my wedding.

Made in the palest shade of lavender, the satin slip dress falls elegantly to the floor with a high split over my right leg. Then, there are the spaghetti straps with a plunging neckline that accentuates the larger breasts the pregnancy left behind as a gift to my male for months of crazy hormones and cravings.

"Are you almost ready? The sun sets in less than five minutes," Gabriella calls out, knocking on the door once while I hear Isa herding the kids out of the room with the help of my mother, who's become super grandmother to all our kids. She loves them and they adore her spoiling ways, but lately, there's a new sparkle in her eye. A change in her, and I wonder why...

Maybe Isa knows? I'll ask her after.

"Just slipping on my dress. I'm almost out." Fixing and adjusting, I check myself in the mirror, and what I see brings a smile to my face. My blonde hair is curled and my makeup is soft, shades of shimmering pink and light purple with a nude, glossy lip and a bit of mascara tie in the look together. I'm beautiful and feel it, too. I'm happy, truly so, and there isn't a single thing left behind of the broken fae princess Leo met a little less than two years ago. "I belong with him."

Tanix and I are waiting, my female. Come to us.

Exiting the bathroom, I pick up a small tiara and hand it to Gabby, who pins it in place and then hugs me before tugging me along behind her. The ceremony is being held on Wiccan grounds, but my people are in attendance along with other close friends. There's an open portal between the two realms; it sits on spacious land with easy access to our home while still being private enough to not intrude on the daily lives of our coven.

Not that they don't love it, because they do. Most take vacations there and have made lifelong friendships with new business opportunities or Friday night board games: a new craze in the fae world.

However, it's the four waiting on my path to Leo, little sunflowers and lilies in their hands, that make me cry. I can't help it. I'm touched by the gesture. More so when Gabriella, who'd rushed to her spot after exiting the house, comes right back and wipes under each eye. She snorts and shakes her head, but then tells me to *buck up* because all the women in the family have been super emotional on their wedding days.

She has a way with words and a bigger heart, and I'm laughing with her between trembling chins and deep breaths to calm down. Her mate is next.

Theodore's never been one for a lot of words, but you know he cares in subtle ways. It's bringing you a present just because, or amusing me when I send him emojis of how Tanix is doing that day or the way he says, "I'm proud of you, little sister."

He hands me his flowers before I can respond and then glares at my tears, which makes me laugh again. It's a vicious cycle that carries over when I notice his lily is blood red, and I don't care that it doesn't fit in with any decoration or theme—the thought counts. He wanted to be a part of my day.

Isa and Xadiel join us next, and the werewolf zooms in on the red flower immediately. "That cheating arsehole." Not the first time I hear it and it won't be the last, but I am amused, as is his wife when he ties a green and gold ribbon around the makeshift bouquet. His mate raises a brow, which he only shrugs to, unashamed of the one-upping games the two men play. "I came prepared, little moon. We know how he is."

Said vampire was right behind me and merely responded with a hiss, my cue to find my male. The calmer of the three, yet just as deadly when you touch what he holds dear.

Up ahead, there's a break in the pathway he created for this day.

At first, we wanted to have our ceremony right away, but then ideas formed. The things we wanted shifted, and having Tanix be a part of this day was something that felt right for Leonardo and me, and we were right.

I find the two most important people in the world standing under the rising moon in their coven colors and with the cutest smiles on their faces. They watch me walk the rest of the way to them while our siblings find their seats, and when I accept my male's hand, I hear it.

That second heartbeat.

He hears it, and the blue eyes that I adore smolder as he wraps his other arm around me and holds his family close. It's a little difficult to have a binding ceremony when the man's hands are occupied and unwilling to let anyone go, so in the end, the ribbon is wrapped around the three of us and the new addition who's decided to say hello from his cozy home inside my womb.

"You've made me the happiest man in the world, Anaya Moore. I will never love or want for another, and when the time comes that the goddess calls us home, I will search for you in the heavens to love you all over again."

EPILOGUE #2
Anaya

FOUR YEARS LATER...

I can't help but smile as I look around the table.

It's full and loud, and add in the occasional growl—can overwhelm at times—but I wouldn't change it for anything in the world. This is us—my family.

Growing up the way I did, this is all I hoped my future could be, but it felt so out of reach. Because of lies. Because of the hurt drilled into me, but then I met my Leonardo.

My heart. My king.

Right now, he's sitting at the head of our dining table with our Tanix in his lap and the latter is digging his chubby fingers into his *papa's* plate. He's our little food pirate, unapologetic and without shame. To make it worse, stealing is the only way to get him to eat, so Leo has two plates: his real one and the fake, baby-approved decoy.

Across from us is Theodore and Gabriella who are visiting with their three kids: Beloved, their firstborn, and then twin boys, Paolo and Alaric, who are just a few months old. She's sitting in a high-chair next to her cousin Atticus, Xadiel and Isa's little boy, while the twins sleep in a portable bed not far from us.

All the male children have their grandfather's name in one manner or another; first or middle.

The werewolf ruler's second child is with me, and the little princess might be attached to her Aunt Aya. Since the day she was born, Thalia's sought me out whenever we'd visit or they'd come here, and that's every week.

Because no matter what's happening or where we are, Sunday dinners have become a human tradition we've adopted. We take turns hosting, making sure to have enough to feed the beast that is Xadiel. His wolf can outeat our entire coven. We do the same for Theodore and Gabriella; their blood is harvested from *ethically-sourced* donors for the *most* part.

No judgment from me whatsoever.

Vampires cannot change their nature any more than I can. No more than a werewolf needs to hunt for his meat, or I crave pixie-berry tarts or a flower petal salad. No more than Isabella craves her coffee, her newest obsession as of the last year.

She has the latest machines, flavored syrups, and frother. An entire section of her kitchen is now dedicated and stocked with anything you could think of to brew the intricate concoctions.

"We have visitors," Isabella says then and reaches over for her daughter. The little sprite wiggles and then crawls across the tabletop for her maman, and that's when I realize she's pushed plates out of the way. At my raised brow, she merely taps her head and I don't argue, just like the rest of the table. The men, who'd been discussing a recent rugby match between Xadiel and Theo's guards a few weeks back, also stop. Silence ensues, just a fraction of a second before three men stand at the end of my dining table.

They appeared out of nowhere.

Tall. Imposing. Powerful.

I won't deny a shiver of fear passing through me; the man on the right killed Larue without exerting any force, and Leo rushes to my side. He hands me Tanix, his stance protective, and all the men do the same.

"Why are you here, Father?" Theo says, and my head snaps in his direction.

What the...? Leo?

My male's warm hand lifts to the back of my neck and cups it, slowly sliding his thumb up and down my pulse point. ***Relax, precious one. He's Thanatos's son, but the relationship is a bit strained; Theo hasn't forgiven him completely yet.***

Because of what happened to Gabby?

Yes. He blames the God of Death for making him wait.

"I've come to see my grandchildren, my son. Gabriella invited me." Theo's eyes flick down to his bride and finds her smiling at him before crooking a finger. A silent request he adheres to, bending at the waist until he's at the right distance for her to lean over and kiss his cheek before nuzzling his jaw. Gabriella doesn't stop until he relaxes. "Did we miss dinner?"

"Why are the other two here?" My brother-in-law's tone isn't the most welcoming, but he is resigned to making his mate happy. And the way she looks at him, that hint of mischief in her reddish eyes after a feed, almost makes me laugh.

I hold it in, but then Xadiel snorts and I can't help the giggle that slips through. The vampire king is a complete softie for his family. To the world, he might be a monster, but for his wife and children, the word *no* just doesn't exist.

"They've come for other reasons." Beloved decides at that moment she's done with her harvest stew made with fresh blood, and with her eyes on Thanatos, the little hybrid lifts her hands in the universal *carry me* sign. And the God of Death melts, a proud Grand-Père if I ever saw one. It's adorable to watch her pat his cheeks and babble while he nods as if it were the most amazing thing he's ever heard.

"Queen Anaya," a dark, yet velvet voice speaks, and my head turns to the man who killed my father. I hold no ill intentions toward him, not at all, but I find this god intimidating. "Do you know who I am, little one?"

I nod. "Ares."

"Correct." Leo takes a step closer, but Ares smiles at him. It's small and looks unnatural on him, but that simple action completely puts me at ease. "I mean no harm, King Moore. Not to her, or any member of the family here present. None of us do."

A gift appears in his hand and as he walks over to our end of the table, I catch sight of the same looking offering appearing in the hands of the two gods who came with Ares. I don't know the third one, but he's now taken a protective stance beside Isabella and hands her a wrapped package. Same with Thanatos to Gabriella, and another for Beloved.

Intricately wrapped, the golden paper shimmers in the room's lighting. They are small, palm-sized, but heavy at the same time.

I shake mine a bit. "Thank you."

"Open it, Anaya. I'll explain after." I try to hand Tanix over to his father and open the gift, but my son surprises me and jumps toward the God of War. Ares catches him without a problem, holding my son with care, and allows him to pull on his hair without so much as grimacing. "Go on, little one. I must leave soon, but—"

"Oh my…" That comes from Isa, and she's looking at the third god with confusion. "Lord Hades, how did I not see this? I don't understand."

"Because I made it so." His voice is deep, yet low. An admonishing whisper. "You need to learn that surprises can be fun, little seer. Nothing wrong with them."

"But what does this mean?" At her question, one by one, the men drop to one knee while maneuvering the children a little higher. With one hand, they keep them secure, and the other goes over their chest. "You three hold favor with the gods. I pledge my protection and loyalty to you, Isabella."

"And I to you, Gabriella," Thanatos says, kissing the side of Beloved's head. "No harm will ever come to you, or your offspring."

"What about your son?"

"He's a demi-god, my daughter. Nothing can touch him without him tearing it apart."

"Anaya?" Ares speaks low, and I have a feeling this calm behavior is not one he's used to. War is never peaceful. "Open it."

"Sorry. Got distracted," I say sheepishly, tearing open the delicate paper and removing the top to a velvet case. "Ares, I—"

"You hold my favor because I've never encountered a being who has no hatred in her heart." Taking the necklace from the box, he gives it to Leo to place around my neck. Leo does so, as do the other men I consider brothers. Each stone is different, but mine is an osten-tatious ruby with diamonds around the teardrop gem. "You've been hurt, yet you do not lash out. You had every right to pray and ask for vengeance, but you only sought justice and peace. For that alone, you will always have my blessing. That, and you're the daug—"

"Anaya, little Miss Ariella is awake and needing a..." Maman trails off, her eyes wide and her lips slightly parted. "What are you doing here, Ares? We talked and agreed that—"

"I need my mate by my side, Amelia. Please come home with me."

Turn the page for an announcement…

NEW SERIES ANNOUNCEMENT

NEW SERIES COMING SOON!

A GOD'S OBSESSION SERIES COMING 2025

ARES & AMELIA
THANATOS & TBA
HADES & TBA

This will not be a retelling, but a love story between a God and his fated mate.
One might be a human, another a fae, and the last…

No Mythology Used.

Living in the Fate's Bite Series world is my happy place; a total dream come true, and the excitement and love you guys have for my characters leave me in total awe. Thank you so much for reading, my peeps!

Each review and all the excitement make my little author's heart pitter-patter!

Up next, is Marcia's book with her Serpentine Prime Alpha. Oh, that man is a fighter and a biter and EVERYTHING. After, in The Hunt, we will play a sexy game of chase. I won't say with whom just yet, but you will LOVE it!!!

The books will be filled to the brim with growly, possessive alpha males and their sassy mates. What to expect:

*Biting
*A lot of Smut
*Literal Touch Her & D.I.E.
*Enemies
*Hunting
*Power Play

Come To Me: 8/12/2024
https://books2read.com/ComeToMe-FatesBite

The Hunt: 10/17/2024
https://books2read.com/The-Hunt-Fates-Bite

SERIES ORDER:
LITTLE LIES
LITTLE MATE
HALF TRUTHS: THEN
HALF TRUTHS: NOW
OMISSION PART ONE
OMISSION PART TWO

SPIN-OFFS:
COME TO ME
THE HUNT

The Beautiful Sinner Series are all interconnected standalones full of suspense and romance and an OTT alpha willing to burn the world to the ground for the woman he loves! It's sexy and has an edge of darkness that will leave you breathless! #MAFIAROMANCE

Now Live!
SIN #1
COVET #2
MINE #3
YOURS #4
RISQUE #5
OWN #6

Beautiful Sinner Spin-Off:
CORRUPT
MY SINFUL VALENTINE
SAVAGE KISS
ONE RULE

ABOUT THE AUTHOR

ELENA M. REYES IS THE EPITOME OF A FLORIDIAN AND IF SHE COULD
LIVE IN HER BELOVED FLIP-FLOPS, SHE WOULD.

As a small child, she was always intrigued by all forms of art:
whether it was dancing to island rhythms, or painting with any
medium she could get her hands on. Her passion for reading over the
years has amassed her with hours of pleasure, but it wasn't until she
stumbled upon fanfiction that her thirst to write overtook her world.

She's a short and sassy Latina with an adorable pup, a kiddo that
keeps her on her toes, and a husband who claims she'll cause him to
go bald prematurely. Lol

Want to keep up to date with Elena's crazy book life?

Follow here:

Website:
https://www.elenamreyes.com/

Find My Books Here:
https://www.bookbub.com/authors/elena-m-reyes

Email:
Reyes139ff@gmail.com

FB Reader Group:
Elena's Marked Girls. Come join the naughty fun.
Link: https://www.facebook.com/groups/1710869452526025/

facebook.com/AuthorElenaMReyes
x.com/ElenaMReyes
instagram.com/elenar139
amazon.com/Elena-M-
Reyes/e/B00E3E26X8/ref=dp_byline_cont_pop_ebooks_1
bookbub.com/authors/elena-m-reyes
tiktok.com/@elenamreyes

ALSO, BY ELENA M. REYES

Taste Of You
Doctor's Orders
Back To You

<u>STANDALONES:</u>

Craving Sugar
Stolen Kisses